Quest for the
Golden Orchid

by Roger Stimson
Illustrated by Johann Schweder Grimstvedt

To order additional copies of this book, contact:
Xlibris
0800-056-3182
www.xlibrispublishing.co.uk
Orders@ Xlibrispublishing.co.uk

ISBN: Softcover   978-1-9845-9144-9
        EBook   978-1-9845-9145-6

Print information available on the last page

Rev. date: 08/29/2019

HERMIA BRISK DESMOND DAZZLE LILLY DOMINIC/DONALD DOUGLAS/DEWIE (VARIATIONS)

BERTHA HO GERTRUDE

'ARRY 'ORACE WILGER FUDDLE SQUIDGE

ANTS FLIT DAMSELFLY EARWIG

The tale is of a bee named Hermia who, while dreaming of adventure, makes an error in the hive. The drones are outraged! To pacify them, the Queen sends Hermia off on a quest to find the pollen of the mysterious Golden Orchid! During her journey to find this rare flower, Hermia has many strange and interesting adventures. Will she succeed? Finally, when she is close to finding the flower, she uncovers a dastardly plot against a hive that has befriended her. Hermia and her friends have to find a way to defend the hive from destruction!

Each of the 15 stories can be read by themselves but we believe they will each make the reader want to read on as the tale develops and becomes more intriguing and exciting in each succeeding chapter! The writing of this set of stories, though essentially for children of 6 years upwards, includes a number of more complex words. However, these are explained in context or directly as part of the comedy/drama. This is designed partly to colour the prose and partly to educate younger people into a wider vocabulary. However, if there is still difficulty, there is a vocabulary at the back of the book. Parents may find they enjoy this story too! Each story ranges between 4 and 10 minutes reading.

Contents

Quest for the Golden Orchid

BOOK ONE

Hermia's Mistake

In which Hermia, the bee, makes a mistake while dreaming of freedom and is caught out by the drones. She must make a penance!

Spring is all a' swirling
Around leaves and buds uncurling;
Amongst insects all a' whirling in the showers.

Oh, the countryside's awakening
And the farmwives are a' baking,
While the farmers' boots, they're
shaking from the bowers.

Hermia

From the glowing logs a' sizzling,
Through the chimney stack a' fizzling,
To where bees are busy quizzing in the flowers,

Only tiny steps arrive,
To the strumming of the hive,
Where a little world's alive in waxen towers.

Bzzz-bzz-bzzzzz...

"What was that Hermione?" *asked Hyacinth bee.*

"I said that is isn't raining now."

"Oh? But Hermia said, only ten minutes ago, that the rain was tumbling – a sadness and a sorrow – from a great, grey, mountainside of a sky."

"Well, that wasn't how Dewi put it earlier," *laughed Hermione.*

Hyacinth peered nervously around the corner of Apple Tree hive to check. "Will it rain again?" *she asked, shaking one leg so that a dewdrop flew like a small balloon through the air behind her, landing, ever-so-delicately, upon a bluebell.*

Hermione lifted her nose confidently and sniffed deeply, "This smells as sweet a day as I can recall. I'm off to a bunch of particularly fragrant daffodils growing in the meadow by the old duck pond. Are you coming?"

Hyacinth emerged carefully from under the sill of the hive, took a deep breath and, tight shutting her eyes, leapt, with all the reckless courage of youth, into the nowhere of the day; into a heady and glorious pursuit of pollen.

Meanwhile, the scene inside the busy hive was quite different. A large bee was organising things: "Come along now, come along, these combs must be finished by midday. A little more wax on the north side, I think, Hilary. DON'T spill the pollen, Harmony, – and, Dudley, do stop leaping behind me as if you had been stung by a wasp."

"Oh, a wasp eh? Oh my, how droll. Oh, very droll, Ma'am, if I may venture to say? Oh, most amusing don't you think children?" *said a particularly official-looking drone. The drone then pushed Dudley roughly behind him.*

Queen Gertrude paused and turned to stare at the drone – for it was the Queen herself who was at this moment overseeing the work.

"Desmond," *she began, speaking very slowly,* "just as it is my duty to say WHAT is to be done, it is your duty to see that it IS done. Is that quite clear?

Queen Gertrude

There, there, Dudley. Are you all right now?" *asked Queen Gertrude, looking at the small drone of whom she was secretly rather fond. She then turned to glare at Desmond.*

"Yes, Your Majesty," *replied the drone as he flew off in a hurry ordering the smaller bees around.*

"Come along now, come along! Harriet, neater than that if you please! Hortensia, not that neatly it will take all day! Hermia, have you finished your five-sided cell yet ...?"

Desmond stopped and stared. "Hermia," *he gasped,* "Hermia ... this ... this ...

THIS CELL HAS ONLY FIVE SIDES," *he shouted and his words echoed around the hive:*

"HAS ONLY FIVE SIDES
ONLY FIVE SIDES!"
FIVE SIDES
SIDES SIDES SIDES?"

Did you say ... did you say five? *repeated Dominic, Donald, Douglas and Dewi as they sped to the scene. But, before Desmond had a chance to remind Hermia of her duty, the others burst in,* "Explain yourself, Hermia! Why has this cell only five sides, ungrateful bee; why has it not six sides like every other cell?" *they cried, as one.*

Hermia's face dropped. "I'm sorry it has upset you," *she whispered tearfully.* "I just thought it would look rather nice!"

"What?! What?! What?! What?! **WHAT?!**
shouted all the drones, in horror.

NICE?!

"Hermia," *began Desmond,* "it is my duty ..."

But the drone got no further, for, at that moment, Queen Gertrude appeared from around the corner.

"What ... but what, my children, is going on here?" *She bellowed.*

Desmond drew himself up to his full height of 2.5 centimetres (although he did not normally think in metric) and, holding up one of his six legs for attention, spoke rather severely:

"I regret, Ma'am, that there appears to be an aberration in this cell!"

"Aberr-what, Desmond?" *asked Gertrude, patiently.*

"Ab-err-ation, ma'am. It means a ... divergence; a... deviation from the norm; the word, ma'am is - 'ahem' - a derivation of the Latin aberro meaning 'I wander away' ... in short," *Desmond offered, feeling that somehow he had just lost the queen's full attention,* "an error, Ma'am!"

"Are you trying to tell me that one of my bees has made a mistake, Desmond?"

"Ah yes, Ma'am, to simplify things somewhat, that is what I am attempting to infer!"

"If so, why didn't you say so in the first place? I demand to hear this all explained to me, very carefully." *Gertrude then sat down to listen. However, this was not so straight-forwards for a queen bee is so very much larger than a worker bee, or even a drone. As a result, they all scattered in different directions.*

"Hrmph!" *snorted Gertrude, as she finally settled down.* "Now, will someone kindly explain the problem to me, slowly and clearly?"

Desmond cleared his throat and began: "It has been drawn to our attention, Ma'am, indeed thrust upon our very senses, that without authority, without precedence and in breach of article 123456 - the necessary article covering the design of the cell, laid down in … erumph … wherever it was laid down ... that a certain young bee has, 'aberrantly'," *he coughed to emphasize the word,* "created an unorthodox geometric shape.

Desmond

That is to say, Ma'am, in short, a certain bee has constructed a pentagon (gasps) instead of the usual, nay statutory, hexagon, Ma'am!" *Desmond then stood back, importantly, waiting for the effect of his words to sink in.*

"Would you believe that?" *whispered Hattie bee.*

"Will someone please tell me what he is talking about?" *demanded Gertrude, looking crossly at Desmond.*

"If you will allow, Ma'am," *explained Donald,* "I think what Desmond is trying to tell us is that one of our worker bees has made a five-sided cell instead of a six-sided cell."

"WHAT?" *shouted Gertrude, pushing them all aside.* "Let me see!" *The queen stared hard at the offending cell.* "He's right, you know. He's quite right!" *Gertrude counted the cell one way, and then she counted it the other. Then she exploded,* "Who, but I mean who is responsible for this … this … this 'aberr' thing?"

All the bees fell silent. There was not a single buzz in the hive. Then, very reluctantly, a small bee was pushed forwards, trembling, out of the huddle, towards the queen.

Queen Gertrude studied the bee up and down very carefully
"Hermia …," *she said finally.* "You do not have five legs, do you?"
"No, Ma'am,"
"No, Hermia. You have six, like any sensible creature. A cell, Hermia, has six sides. It always had six sides; it has six sides; it always will have six sides.

Look around you, Hermia. As the rules demand, all my cells, you will notice, have six sides, each one and, whilst I have the breath to count them, they will indeed continue to have six sides. Will you please explain to me why, on the other hand, your 'aberr' thing has only five sides?"

Hermia began to cry. "Oh, Ma'am, it isn't fair. All the other bees go out every day collecting pollen for the honey. Why, there they are with the wind in their wings and the sunshine on their noses. They can alight upon a flower ... if so the mood takes them. Indeed, Ma'am, they can see a host of golden daffodils if they are lucky. But I, poor Hermia must stay inside every day, Ma'am, just building cells; each one exactly the same as the other; six sides here, six sides there, six sides everywhere ma'am. I felt trapped so I ... so there it is, you see." *Hermia looked appealingly at the queen for support.*

"I see," *murmured Gertrude (not seeing at all).* "I do see how you might feel, Hermia, but that does not explain actually making a five-sided cell instead of our beautiful and, need I say it, thoroughly practical six-sided cells! Hmmn?"

"Ohhh," *wailed Hermia,* "it's just that I become dreamy and restless. Wild thoughts rise in my breast. I don't know what to do with myself. I become kind of skittish and things begin to happen to me, Ma'am, if you please."

"She becomes what, Desmond?" *asked Gertrude, quite alarmed.*

"I believe," *explained the drone,* "that Hermia is indicating, albeit erratically, ma'am, that at certain moments, whose origin, ahem, remains temporarily unexplained, her normal sensory functions are in some way impaired ... Ma'am!"

"What is the matter with you, Desmond? Are you doing this deliberately? Dominic, will you explain?"

"I'm not sure I can, Your Majesty," *said Dominic kindly.*

"That's more like it," *smiled the queen,* "now I understand. What you are trying to say, my dear, is that you become dreamy and restless and don't know what to do with yourself. Isn't that it?"

"I am sure I couldn't have put it better myself, Ma'am," *replied Hermia, shyly.*

"That, Hermia is why I am Queen and you … you are just a dear child. Look at her my children," *said Gertrude pointing her out to all the bees now crowded around her.* "Can you not see that, from her honey sack to her feelers, the poor thing is restless and unfulfilled?" *The queen sat for a time pondering, while all the bees studied Hermia's honey sack and feelers for the tell-tale signs of 'unfulfillment'.*

Hermia

Suddenly the large bee jumped up. Well, that is to say, she heaved herself upright, so that Dudley, who had nestled up close to her, was bowled head over heels onto the floor of the hive.

"I, Queen Gertrude, daughter of Queen Ermintrude, granddaughter of Queen Charlotte, great-granddaughter of Queen Lolita (poor dear)," *began Gertrude, in great ceremony,* "have the solution. Come to me, Hermia, and listen to what I have to say."

Hermia moved closer to the large bee, her eyes wide.

"It is many springs, Hermia, since there was a telling of that mystery which has ever been told to young bees. Your mention of golden daffodils has brought it to mind." *Gertrude then spoke in a loud voice so that all of the hive could hear what she was about to say.* "You, Hermia, will go on a journey. You will find the pollen of the famed Golden Orchid!" *She paused for effect.* "And you will bring it back to us, here! "There, what do you think of that, then?"

Hermia gulped. "But isn't that just an old story, Ma'am?" *she asked, wishing now that she had never foolishly built a five-sided cell or spoken the way she had.*

"I doubt it, Hermia," *said Gertrude, stiffly.* "Now, be a good bee and get yourself prepared. Go along now."

Without thinking and with her wings drooping sadly, Hermia struggled to the edge of the hive. She turned for one last look at all her childhood friends who stared at her with awe. Closing her eyes tight shut, Hermia took a deep breath and simply leapt into the fearful, free, wide and wonderful open air.

"Hermia," called Gertrude after her... but she had gone. Hermia had left the hive; had flown into the wild blue yonder, away from familiar voices and

all the memories she had grown up with. Hermia was far from authority and advice. She was alone, terrifyingly alone! Hermia was free ....

"Oh the foolish child," *said Gertrude.* "I forgot to tell her which way to go. I do hope she will be alright."

She gazed into the distance, trying still to see the little bee while tutting to herself, in concern. Then, quickly bringing herself back to the hive, she bellowed, "Come along, come along now! Get those combs under way, and, Dudley, if I catch you there once more I'll send you in search of the deadly dung beetle."

"Oh, I say," *Hattie blurted out,* "I heard that!"

Quest for the Golden Orchid

BOOK TWO

The Red Admiral

In which Hermia meets her first stranger - a rather interesting butterfly!

Oh a butterfly is a balmy fly;
He flutters to and fro
And, if you watch, you've no idea
Where he intends to go.

He sits upon a cabbage leaf -
No point in saying shoo
- Until he flutters off again
To sing 'taroo, taroo.'

Brisk

The early morning haze seemed, to Hermia, like a magical veil as she made her way through the fields in her Royal Quest for the Golden Orchid.

The bobbing of the mayfly amongst a wild profusion of poppies – their colours waving like a troupe of clowns jesting in the cornfields leant a hypnotic quality to the scene. This, and the scent of a thousand wildflowers wafting on the morning breeze, made Hermia want to sneeze. Soon she began to feel drowsy … She was buzzing along happily when, all of a sudden, she very ALMOST bumped into a large and brightly coloured butterfly.

Hermia swerved as the butterfly veered crazily. Catching his breath, he landed on a Blue Cornflower shouting, "Avast there, swab the decks, and ahoy mate; what's going on here? What's the meanin' of all this dash, eh? Can't a sailor have a peaceful morning without some young feller-me-lad knocking him out of the skies?"

"I'm sorry, sir," *said Hermia, gazing curiously at the Red Admiral Butterfly.*

"Sorry sir? Sorry sir? Don't y' know that steam gives way to sail, sir? I was most definitely sailing and ... if I may say so, sir ... you seemed most definitely to be steamin'! Can't y' see me rank eh? Admiral, that's it, Admiral Brisk that's me, sir. What? What are you doing here, anyway?"

"I don't know, sir!"

"You don't know, sir? You don't know, sir? Well what do y' know then? Speak up, quickly now"

"Oh er, I know how to recite poetry – and she began.

"As I went to Bonner,
I met a pig
Without a wig
Upon my honour!"

"Quite," *said the butterfly simply,* "anything else?"

"Not really. I am searching for something!"

"Ah, what's that? What's that? … ahumph?" *asked the admiral, puffing out his chest.* "Ah, maybe I can be of assistance, eh?"

"Well you see," *said Hermia, going through her story so far,* "I used to look after the cells …"

At this the Admiral flinched. "Cells was that? Cells eh! Oh, deary me, cells! This could be a police officer by the sounds of it – and here, no doubt, directin' the traffic! "Ah, now I can see you are clearly an officer and a gentleman, sir. But what's the rush, my hearty? National importance? No doubt! Chasin' some criminal … or perhaps even a spy, eh? Curious combination, a poet and police officer," *he muttered to himself.* "Well, well, you were, of course, simply directing the traffic, I am sure. Do accept my sincere apologies, old chap."

Hermia blinked as the Admiral waved his arms about dramatically.

"Blot on my copybook, eh? Daresay you'll give me a ticket, but look here officer, the sun is a bit blindin' today ... a fellow can get a bit dazed ... obviously jumped the lights ... mistook a marigold for a greengage, eh? Easily done, what?"

"That's quite alright," *said Hermia,* "I wasn't really paying attention, myself.

"Look here," *interrupted the Admiral;* "Y' know how it is when you're in a certain position ... these cabbage whites ... one bit of gossip and it's all over the cabbage patch. Well, how about it? Not a word, eh? Not a word?"

"Of course, not a word," *echoed Hermia, quite bewildered.* "Not a word to anyone."

Brisk smiled broadly and slapped Hermia heartily on the back.

"Awfully grateful," *he whispered.* "Now, I have some particularly spicy raspberry wine; rescued it from a vinegar fly last Wednesday. You must drop round sometime and take a glass ... er when you're off duty, eh? Must be off now ... have an important engagement ... nice to meet you. Toodle pip!"

"Toodle – er goodbye," *said Hermia, staring, as the Red Admiral wobbled very unsteadily on his way, looking, for all the world, as if he had already tasted some of his raspberry wine.*

"Oh dear," *sighed Hermia,* "I forgot to ask him if he knew where I might find the Golden Orchid. What shall I do now?" *and, curling up on the cornflower, she fell fast asleep, dreaming of fleets of butterflies reciting poetry and drinking gallons of raspberry wine.*

Quest for the Golden Orchid

BOOK THREE

Hermia and the Ants

Bureaucracy (can you say this?) is a word that few like. It is much to do with keeping notes about everything and making sure everything is done by certain rules. Here, Hermia encounters bureaucracy as organised by the ants!

An ant, it rushes back and forth
And back and forth again.
Then it stands quite still
In case you catch it at its game!

As Hermia was dozing in the morning sunshine, lying upon the blue Cornflower, she was now dreaming of tall sailing ships, manned by fierce butterflies floating in an ocean of raspberry wine. It was on one particularly high wave that she felt a slight tickling sensation on the end of her nose! She snorted and she blew and, finally, she opened one eye to find a rather official looking ant, who appeared to be wearing thin wire spectacles, waving a piece of paper in her face.

"What are you doing here? What is your job? Who are you? Why are you here? Do you have the necessary authority to sleep on this Cornflower? And why don't you answer?" *squeaked the ant.*

Hermia opened the other eye and looked down at the ant. "I beg your pardon?" *she asked, yawning stiffly while the ant repeated the questions without any change of tone. Hermia noticed that, behind the first ant, there was a long line of other ants, each one holding a similar sheet of paper.*

"Do you understand the question?" *asked the ant, patiently.*

"It is not the questions that are difficult to understand but your reason for asking them!"

"Oh, that is no problem, I am an official, you see. Officials are supposed to ask questions. You are supposed to answer, and then the officials write the answers on little pieces of paper which are filed away somewhere. Is that clear now?"

"Well, I was sleeping, as you ask" *answered Hermia, amused by such a strange idea.*

"I see," *continued the ant,* "and how long have you been sleeping here?"

"I'm not really sure!"

"Do you sleep here more often, less often, rarely or never?"

"Is it really important?"

"I must have all the necessary information -" *insisted the ant* "- for the files you see! After all, if everyone were to start sleeping on cornflowers whenever they felt like it, the place would be swarming with sleeping bees – wouldn't it! Oh, did you hear that … 'swarming' … with bees!"

Hermia tried to picture bees swarming while asleep, but gave up.

"Well, if it will make your job easier, I am resting on my journey."

"We haven't got to the bit about why, yet," *snapped the ant, remembering his dignity.* "Please answer the question!"

By this time Hermia was feeling a bit stiff, so she moved her leg.

At this sudden movement, the ant jumped back in terror. Seizing her opportunity, Hermia put on a fierce expression.

"Just a moment, small ant," *she cried, in a loud voice,* "by what authority do you ask these questions of an envoy of Queen Gertrude of Apple Tree Hive?"

At this, the ant took a step backwards.

Ants

"Oh dear," *he moaned,* "I am getting everything wrong today. First, I tried to accuse a butterfly of being drunk … he was singing, you know, and wobbling about in a most unusual manner. How was I to know that he was really a famous opera singer? And now I question a Royal messenger! I shall surely be questioned about this, myself! Oh my, oh my!"

"Oh, just find me someone who knows the area will you?" *said Hermia, smiling to herself and wondering if Admiral Brisk was indeed an admiral, or an opera singer, neither or both!* "and we will forget all about it."

"Thank you thank you thank you," *said the ant, bowing low.*

And all the other ants echoed him, saying, "Thank you thank you thank you thank you…" *all the way down the line.*

Very quickly he disappeared down the stem of the flower, to look for a guide.

It was not long before the little ant returned, with a flying ant, to direct Hermia.

The flying ant looked at Hermia "I am most awfully sorry for this confusion, madam," *and, glowering at the little ant.* "How may I help you?"

"At last," *sighed Hermia,* "good manners!" *and the little ant shrunk down, even further.* "I am searching for the Golden Orchid. Do you know of it? This is a quest given me by Queen Gertrude, Herself!"

"Ah -" *murmured the flying ant* "One has indeed heard of such a queen but, sadly, one is ignorant of the whereabouts of this flower."

Hermia was completely entranced by the flying ant's way of speaking and said nothing.

"However," *continued the flying ant,* "were one to wait until nightfall, perhaps on a branch nearer the woods, one may be able to hail a passing firefly who, without a doubt, will take one to our most brilliant moth, Professor Dazzle. Why, only recently he stated, after spending just two hours circling around what someone had rashly called a candle, that one should never jump to conclusions and that it might, or might not be the moon, but that one could not possibly tell for certain until one had made the proper tests! There, what do you think of that?"

"Very impressive!" *replied Hermia, feeling that was what she was expected to say.*

She then thanked the ant and flew off to the woods and onto a branch to wait for night time. There she fell asleep, to the tapping of a thousand small typewriters.

Quest for the Golden Orchid

BOOK FOUR

Professor Dazzle's Advice

Hermia meets Professor Dazzle who is a moth and a scientist.
(He speaks with a little bit of a German accent!)

'Upon my word!' the moth declared,
'Zis is a sticky vicket;
The moon's gone down behind a cloud
Und I'm in a shady thicket!'

It was evening. The moon shimmered in her silver evening gown. She danced, barefoot, across the shadowy fields and rippled across the lake to swim, for one delightful moment, on the back of a golden carp. Then, tossing her long moonbeam strands of hair behind her, she skipped lightly amongst the daisies, sighed and rested her elbows upon the branch of an old oak tree while one small moonbeam skipped off to peek, cheekily, at Hermia, still fast asleep on the blue cornflower.

Hermia awoke with a start..."Oh! The Golden Orchid ... Professor Dazzle ... I must find them! Now, what did the ant say? 'If you want to find this rare flower first ask a firefly to direct you to the moth, who declares he knows everything worth knowing!'"

The bee cleaned her whiskers, thoughtfully, wondering where she might find a firefly, when, all of a sudden, a small light whizzed past!

"Hey, you there! Wait a minute, I want to ..." *But the firefly was gone.* "Just a minute ..." *as another flew past.* "Excuse me ..." *but it was too late.* "It's no good I will just have to be firmer!"

And so, as the next firefly was darting in front of her, she grabbed one of its legs.

"Ouch!" *yelled the firefly.* "Why did you do that?"

Flit

"I am very sorry," *said Hermia,* "but it was the only way to attract your attention!"

"Very funny way of asking! Oh well, now we are both here, please let me go and tell me what you want to know!"

"I need to find Professor Dazzle!" *Hermia almost shouted.*

"You don't need to shout either," *twittered the firefly.* "He's in the woods. And, since you didn't ask, my name is Flit"

"That is very sweet of you, Flit. I am so sorry I was rough with you, but, you see, I am all alone on an urgent mission for Queen Gertrude of Apple Tree Hive."

"Oh well," *said Flit, feeling suddenly very important,* "in **that** case I will take you there. Follow me!"

And the pair flew off into the woods.

Hermia kept close to the little firefly, as her eyesight wasn't so good in the dark, but she had to fly slowly to do so. They found the professor sitting on a rotten branch muttering to himself:

"Very good ... very good, my dears, you little voodlice! Vat it is you chew up ze little pieces of rotten wood like so, ho yes, charming, quite charming."

Professor Dazzle turned to see the pair hovering behind him. "Why hello, Flit, my dear, can you see how zey take ze little pieces of vood and chew zem up so small? Vat you tink eh? Und who is dis friend vat you 'ave wit you?"

"Actually" *answered Hermia, determined not to get caught up in a lecture on woodlice,* "I am commanded by Queen Gertrude of Apple Tree Hive to find something very important and I have been told you know everything."

"Vell, not quite everything, my dear," *smiled the moth;* "just a little more than little fellows like Flit here, eh, Flit?"

"Oh you know everything, Professor D. You wait, miss, you'll see."

"But are you sure you vouldn't rather ask me about ze little voodlice?"

"Another time perhaps, Professor," *replied Hermia, gently,* "I am searching for a very rare and valuable flower and I am told you may know where I can find it."

"A flower, eh?" *mused the moth sadly.* "I am so sorry, my dear, but you must realise that while flowers bloom in the daytime, a moth, even a moth with a degree in curiosity, only comes out at night!"

Hermia's face fell. "Oh, of course," *she murmured,* "how silly of me!"

"Well, perhaps instead, I can offer you my famous cure for Monday mornings!"

"What cure is that?" *asked Hermia, innocently.*

"Vy it is so simple, my dear," *beamed the professor;* "you simply start vork on a Tuesday. Ho ho. Do you get it, eh?"

Flit looked at Hermia and grinned, "He is quite crazy when he is not being clever, you know."

"And I am getting no nearer to the Golden Orchid," *sighed Hermia.*

"Oh do not sigh, my dear," *murmured the moth,* "zere is anozer one who is equally crazy, but he is also said to be very wise. He seems to know many strange things. Sometimes I vunder if he makes it up, but many speak highly of him." *The moth seemed to be studying something.*

"Yes?" *asked Hermia,* "but what is his name?"

"His name? Oh yes, of course. He is called Ho. They call him The Wise Green Dragonfly – but I must say this has not yet been proved! He lives in a pond by the old swamp. Ask Ho he might just know." *And the moth fluttered off muttering to himself* "I vunder if I vere to add just a pinch of parsley to two pinches of… no zat vould not work… vat about…" *Hermia watched as the slightly mad professor drifted off into the night – wondering about this and that.*

"Oh dear, cried Hermia. Flit has gone too. What shall I do now?"

Quest for the Golden Orchid

BOOK FIVE

Fuddle's Muddle

Hermia meets a slightly suspicious horsefly, Fuddle, who tries, cunningly, to lead her deeper into the swamp!

There's little to say.
I shall not try
To assess the merits
Of a coarse horsefly!

Fuddle

The night was aflame with stars, but the bright orb of the moon outshone them all. She still seemed very interested in Hermia's quest for the rare flower, though she winked every so often behind a cloud so that Hermia, unused to flying at night, would gasp and shudder as all manner of wild and weird insects loomed up in front of her. They appeared as monsters to her with their long legs, their large as lamp eyes and the awkward, and seemingly aimless fluttering of their wings.

'Must I go into the swamp?' *Hermia thought to herself.* 'Do I have to go into this dank and gloomy place? *The dank and gloomy place squelched and slopped in her ears. The stench seeped from putrid pools and slimy wastes. Sounds dropped like plump beetles from the damp leaves where the air was as still as listening, not moving unless sucked in or slobbered out by the old careless swamp itself. Was this truly the way? Must she …?*

Hermia alighted upon a reed. Perhaps if she waited, here on the edge of the swamp, Ho The Wise green Dragonfly would find her …

She fell fast asleep. When she awoke she heard a curious noise behind her:

"Fuzz-fuzz-fuzz," *went the noise.* "All work and no play makes Fuddle a dull boy, it does. Oh, it does that all right, fuzz-fuzz-fuzz."

Hermia turned slowly to find a striped insect sitting on the reed, next to her.

"Who are you?" *she asked.* "You are not a dragonfly, are you?"

The answer was indignant: "A dragonfly? Me? Fuddle, who is famed throughout the h'entire horse-racing world, a dragon-fly?"

The voice became higher, "Is Fuddle, who rode upon three successive winners at H'Aintree and who is respected worldwide for his h'unsurpassed knowledge of horses, – a d-r-a-g-o-n-f-l-y? No, Miss Bee, indeed he is not a dragonfly! Fuddle is a horsefly, is Fuddle. Most definitely a h-o-r-s-e-f-l-y!"

Hermia was, by now, aware that she had offended this insect and quickly changed the subject: "Do you live near here? Or are you just visiting?"

"Live HERE?" *echoed the horsefly, with disdain.* "Live here with this motley collection of frogs and toads? Me, Fuddle, live in this stagnant excuse for a pond? No, miss, I do not live here. The conversation here is not about horses, you know, and the only rush you might experience here is not the rush of wind as you are racing down the turf, just stopping yourself from taking a nip at the beast before it reaches the winning post. No, the only rush you find here, miss, is a bulrush. Ho ho, get it, bull-rush, eh? Oh, never mind."

"May I ask why you are here then?" *demanded Hermia, amused by his rough charm.*

"I was afraid you might ask that …" *answered the fly miserably … and said nothing more.*

"Well?" *insisted the bee.*

"Oh, it is a trifling matter and not one I am keen to recall!"

"Come along, Fuddle," *Hermia insisted,* "tell it all!"

"Oh well, as you insist. By some misfortune, I lost a small sum betting on a horse! So I am in the way of taking a lift from a Shetland Pony here to this … this … pond to see someone who may … er … make the loss good, so to speak."

"Do you mean to tell me that the world renowned Fuddle lost a race?" *Hermia asked mischievously.*

"There you are you see," *he sulked,* "I knew you would laugh, and that is what they will all do when I do not arrive for the steeplechase at Goodwood. They will say, slyly, 'Where is Fuddle? Why is he not ridin' the winner? Is he afraid? Has Fuddle lost his nerve?' They will ask. "Oh, the talk … the gossip!" *he wailed.*

Hermia suddenly felt quite sorry for the insect and offered some advice:

"You might always say that you decided to stay in the country to search for new talent in the field of horses!" *she suggested.*

Fuddle looked the bee up and down and replied: "Research you say? Research? Oh, I like that, I do. In fact, that is reasonably clever for a young bee," *he added carelessly.* "I do believe that will serve. But what," *he asked suspiciously,* "can I do for you in exchange for your silence? So long as it isn't of a – ahem - financial nature feel free to call on me. Fuddle's the name but not the brain. Ho ho".

Hermia winced at his rhyming but dared not lose the opportunity of gaining information. "There is just one thing I need. Do you happen to know where Ho, The Wise Green Dragonfly is? I must ask his help in an important matter!"

Fuddle's eyes narrowed when he heard this. "Important matter is that? Important you say? Why, what could possibly be important around here? If you were to tell me more of this 'important matter' I may be able to help you, myself, my dear. After all, you know how vague dragonflies is!"

"Dragonflies are vague?" *echoed Hermia, innocently.*

"Why, you mean you don't know how vague dragonflies is? Oh, my dear, dragonflies is exceedingly vague. Dragonflies is so exceedingly vague that you never know where they are when you are looking for them. Isn't that so?"

"Well, yes it does seem to be so," agreed Hermia.

"Oh, dragonflies is so extremely and so exceedingly vague, my dear," *insisted the horsefly,* "that you don't even know where they are going if you happen to find them, do you?"

"Well, certainly I don't know that yet," *agreed Hermia, rather feeling that she was being pushed.*

"Oh, dragonflies is so very and so extremely vague," *persisted the horsefly,* "that even they don't know where they are going once you have taken the trouble to find them. Oh, don't put your faith in dragonflies miss, they is so terribly unreliable. No, no, you just listen to Fuddle here and he will help you."

"Oh, dear," *thought Hermia, by now thoroughly confused and almost convinced.*

"Now … Miss er … hmmm … to the matter in hand," *Fuddle coaxed Hermia, almost dribbling at the mouth.* "I, Fuddle, shall quite unselfishly put all else aside to help you in this, ahem, important matter. It is important, isn't it?" *he asked persuasively.*

"Oh, it is highly important," *agreed Hermia.*

"Highly important ..." *the fly echoed.*

"Well, perhaps I can trust you a little, after all you are here ..."

"And the dragonfly isn't," *added Fuddle rubbing his legs together gleefully.*

"Oh all right then," *Hermia cried.* "I am searching for a very valuable golden flower for my queen!"

Fuddle had been leaning so far forwards that he almost fell on his nose. Looking up he repeated the words slowly: "Did you say 'valuable ... golden ... flower'?"

"Yes I did," *said Hermia, innocently.* "So you see how very important it is!"

"Thank goodness I found you in time, my dear," *Fuddle blurted out, quite unable to believe his luck.* "Now whoever told you to ask a dragonfly about such an important matter as this?"

"Why, a very respected professor of woodlice told me; a famous moth, Professor Dazzle himself!"

"Oh my, oh my, oh dear, oh dear – a moth told you? A mere moth? A moth who studies woodlice? Well, no wonder you couldn't find this dragonfly," *laughed the horsefly.* "Ho ho, a moth, oh deary me, a moth!"

By now Hermia was completely convinced she had made a mistake and turned to the horsefly, "But what would you do, kind horsefly?" *she asked, by now seriously worried.*

Fuddle was fuzzing away to himself and trying to hide his excitement. "There is but one person who can help you, my dear," *he said slyly;* "a most knowin' gentleman 'e is. 'E goes by the name of Mr 'orentious Squidge and 'e is a mosquito of high intelligence 'e is, miss ... and fine sensitivity. In fact 'e 'as 'is nose in everything, I should think. Well, 'e would you see, bein' as 'e is a gnat, now wouldn't 'e ... eh?"

"This Mr Squidge, you say he can help me on my quest?" *asked Hermia, by now almost completely taken in.*

"Can 'e 'elp you, my dear? Can Mayor Squidge 'elp you? Why, 'e 'elps 'imself pretty well most of the time, doesn't 'e? So I should think 'e can 'elp you, my dear, wouldn't you?"

"Where can I find the – er - gentleman?" *gulped Hermia.*

"Well now, doesn't 'e live at Dock Leaf Mansions, Little Nettles, The Swamp? But make sure you speak to Wilger first. Wilger sort of keeps an eye on things over there."

"Wilger?"

"Just you keep going past that patch of toadstools, over there, till you come to a gorse bush. Then say, in a loud voice: 'The moss grows on the North side of the tree'. Dear old Wilger will find you and help you kindly on your way. Now don't delay, Mr Squidge is a very busy gnat!"

"Past those toadstools, you say?" *she repeated, turning her nose up at the smell.*

"That's it, my dear. You surely aren't afraid of a few old toadstools, are you? And make sure you won't forget to say that Fuddle sent you, will you now?"

"Oh er no, I won't. Thank you, Mr er Fuddle."

At that, the horsefly lifted on the wing and fuzzed away into the swamp in the other direction.

Hermia sniffed at the toadstools. "They don't smell sweet at all. I am not sure I trust this Fuddle!" *she muttered, and she flew straight back into the sunshine to think it all through again.*

Quest for the Golden Orchid

BOOK SIX

Wilger the Wasp

Hermia is captured by the villains in the swamp! How will she escape?

She couldn't have born it
If another large hornet
Had flown quite so close to her head;
For that insect's sting
Is a troublesome thing
That could possibly send you to bed!

It was long into the morning. The sun's warmth had already lifted the early glistening dew into a fine vapour. By now thoroughly refreshed, Hermia, the young bee on her Royal Quest to find the pollen of the Golden Orchid, dipped up and down as she searched for the Wise Green Dragonfly. Ho, she had been told, would know where the Golden Orchid was. Hermia had decided to change her mind about looking for 'Mr Horentious Squidge'. Something inside her warned that Fuddle, the horsefly, was just a little bit too keen to send her there and she simply did not like the sound of his swamp one little bit.

The bee glided over the tops of the waving grasses, sometimes fast and low, sometimes, with a steady hum, she rose higher and higher up into the blue haze following the banks of the lake which shone below her in the sunshine. The heat was beginning to make her feel drowsy again and a little light-headed. It was on one particularly long glide, towards a large clump of bright yellow gorse, that Hermia suddenly heard the hum of beating wings. As she turned to look, the words which exploded in her ears were definitely not the gentle sounds of the Wise Green Dragonfly! No, not at all!

"Well now, 'oo do we got 'ere then, 'Arry?" *thundered the voice.* "Is it an 'overfly would you surmise?"

Hermia found herself staring up into the eyes of a large hornet – a fearsome and dangerous insect if aroused.

'Arry   'Orace

"Oo no, 'Orace, oo no I don't think so, not the way it was flutterin' up and down like what it didn't know what it was doin' or where it was goin'! No, I think it is some kind of a moth!"

"Ah, you might be right there, 'Arry," *replied the other.* "P'raps it's a Tiger Moth eh? Why don't we ask it?"

Having finished their introduction to Hermia, the two ugly hornets just stared at her. Then the larger one spoke again: "May I ask what a young bee is a-doin' of flyin' around in such a huncontrolled manner in this – ahem – peaceful little neighbourhood of ours? Hmmmmmn?"

"Well, I suppose that is a reasonable question for a landowner to ask," *replied Hermia cautiously as she glanced around her looking for a way of escape.*

"Did you 'ear that, 'Arry? A 'landowner'? Hee hee, A reasonable question'? Ho ho! I should say it is reasonable, my young bee. I'd say it was very reasonable, wouldn't you, 'Arry?"

"Didn't strike me as hunreasonable, 'Orace,"

"Reasonable or not I am waitin' for a hanswer. Do you s'pose you know whose territory this is, my young bee?"

Hermia

Hermia looked nervously about her. Then she realised that, by going around the lake, she had ended up in the very place she had been trying to avoid – the old swamp!

"Is it," *she asked thickly,* "by any chance," *she whispered,* "the place where the moss grows on the North side of the tree?"

"Stop!" *rasped a voice behind her.* "I 'eard that I did."

WILGER

At that a rather large wasp with a scarred face and a patch over one eye leant out from a leaf, put up one leg, and, from a jaw dripping with some sticky food, said:

"Ooissheanwarrasshewan?"

"'Allo, Mr Wilger," *said Horace proudly, stepping back.* "I think we have caught a deliberate trespasser – a foreign bee, what doesn't know where she is goin'! I expect Mr Squidge will be pleased with us, won't he, Mr Wilger?"

"Pleased?" *Wilger rasped* "Did I hear you say 'pleased', young Horace? 'Cos if you did then I have serious doubts as to your intelligence! Pleased, to know that a trespasser got this far before bein' stopped? And another thing young Horace, if the bee didn't know where it was goin' how could it be deliberately trespassin', eh? Oh no, my lad, you will 'ave to be quicker than that if you want to please his worship the mayor."

"I'm sorry, Mr Wilger," *the hornet stuttered.* "She came out o' the sun, like, before we could see 'er. But we did get 'er in the end, didn't we, 'Arry?"

"That's enough!" *Interrupted the wasp.* "But wasn't it the password I 'eard 'er come out with? And if it was the password, then she ain't a trespasser, is she young 'Orace? No, she is an ally, ain't she!"

Horace the hornet scratched his head with one feeler. "I s'pose so Wilger!"

"You suppose so, Wilger, do you?" Well, let us suppose no longer and ascertain ..."

"Pardon?" *said Harry.*

"Find out, young Harold, find out!" *The wasp rubbed his legs together to warm himself.* "This, gentlemen, is where subtlety is called for (cunning to you young Harold); not your brute force, but tactics, clever plans," *Wilger emphasised the last words by tapping his nose. Then, hitching up the belt around his large belly he turned to Hermia.*

"Right then, bee," *he snarled* "oo do you know and whaddayouwant? This 'ere is Squidge's patch - Mayor Squidge to you, and 'ere only Squidge gets a bite of all the action. Get it? Get it? 'E's a mosquito see – gets a bite…see? Ha ha." *The wasp's great belly wobbled as he laughed at his own joke, but Hermia was unimpressed.*

"Well I am here on business and Horentius will be most annoyed if you keep him waiting, won't he!" *Said Hermia, slyly.*

Wilger went a little pale at this. "You called him Horentius …you know 'im then?"

"Oh Dock Leaf Mansions is not my idea of a palace, but I suppose it suits the Mayor all right. He doesn't change. As you say he likes to know just what is going on! He doesn't like people wasting his time …does he!"

Wilger looked suspiciously at Hermia. "Business, you say? OK, come on then you lot. Let's get going," *he ordered.* "You too bee," *he yelled as Hermia tried to move off to the side.* "I'm not leaving you!"

And the four of them roared off into the swamp without a backwards glance.

BOOK SEVEN

Horentious Squidge

Hermia enters the headquarters of the villains and meets the mosquito, Horentious Squidge!

A gnat's a gnat
And that is that.
He always appears
When you're lying quite flat!
So what can you do
(if you don't go kersplat)?
Why, show him the door
And give him his hat!

"Eenie meanie miny mo
Whatever it is then I'm in the know.
But if I don't like you off you go
Eenie meanie miny mo!"
Whined a thin voice from the middle of a large patch of stinging nettles.

Squidge

"I'm ever so popular because of my purse and because everyone around me" *The small insect scowled and turned his head slowly* ... " ...is so VERY MUCH WORSE!"

Horentius Squidge, master mosquito, laughed shrilly at this appalling rhyme.

His laughter echoed strangely. This was the only sound, other than the eerie and resonant drip and drop, the slip and slap of sudden slippery surfaces which slid, slopped and slurped in the sweaty old swamp; the silence usually broken only by the occasional bellied croak of an old toad, or the regular rasp of crickets. The small voice, piped, not by chance, through a tall reed, sounded like an old gramophone record playing an ancient tune.

"Eenie meanie miny mo!"

All of a sudden, a rather fierce, very red, ladybird with three spots, landed on a dock leaf right next to the owner of the voice. Without wasting a moment, she began to brush him with a dandelion seed, at the same time as telling him about one of her relations:

"You know my sister Flo?" *she began.*

"You know, Hory, the one with a yellow coat and five dots?"

"No!" *muttered Squidge.*

"Well, anyway," *the ladybird continued, ignoring his rudeness,* "she flew off the other day and she hasn't been seen since!"

"So Flo flew did she?" *Squidge sniggered.* "Wise insect!"

"What did you say?" *bellowed Lilly crossly.* "I said – er – why – er – since – er – yet? Lilly!" *mumbled Squidge, trying to avoid the ladybird's fierce glare.*

Lilly squinted back at the gnat. "That doesn't make sense!" *she said triumphantly, while watching the insect squirm. Squidge mentioned something about the weather and then his snout quivered.*

"Your snout just quivered!" *said the ladybird, pointing straight at it.*

"That means something is about to happen, perhaps a rainstorm. This, I'll have you know," *he said, pointing at his snout,* "is a highly sensitive instrument!"

At that moment, without warning, Squidge went quite rigid. His nose pointed high in the air and, as his legs began to buckle, he ducked quickly around the dock leaf, tripping over Lilly on the way. Poor Lilly rolled off the leaf and, becoming tangled up with the dandelion seed, fell right into a muddy patch at the bottom of the stem shouting:

"You … you great bully you!" *Then she burst into tears and flew off.*

Squidge looked at her disappearing form in the distance with a puzzled look. Then he turned back … terrified … towards the fearsome buzzing which was getting louder and louder … nearer and nearer. Squidge, for all his blustering and bullying, was really a very cowardly insect. His little legs rattled against one another, and a small bead of sweat ran down his long snout, balancing on the end, till it hung trembling in a large round globule. His eyes began to cross as he watched the drop of water,

Lilly

fascinated and horrified, waiting for the 'PLIP' which would echo through the swamp like the firing of a canon ball telling everyone where he was!

BZZZZZZZZZZ

BZZZZZZZZZZZZ

BZZZZZZZZZZZZZZZ

BZZZZZZZZZZZZZZZZZZZ

went the noise.

………………."Plip," *went Squidge.*

Wilger, Harry and Horace, with Hermia in tow, hovered suspiciously over the dock leaf.

"Where is 'e?" *demanded Horace.*

"P'raps he's thinking!" *suggested Harry.*

"What'll 'e be thinkin' about?" *whispered Horace.*

"Shut up and listen," *snapped Wilger.*

They all listened, but all they could hear was a tiny wheezing sound from just below them.

"He was right down in the dumps when I saw him yesterday," *muttered Wilger.*

"P'raps he's still there!" *offered Harry.*

"Oh, right. Well, I must be going. I can't wait around here all day," *said Hermia, hopefully.*"You will tell him I called, won't you!"

"Come back 'ere bee!" *rasped the wasp. But, as he pulled Hermia down onto the dock leaf, the movement knocked Squidge on the head. Squidge, losing his balance toppled off, down and down, into the muddy patch from which Lilly had recently fled in tears.*

"You great blundering idiots!" *came the furious voice of Squidge.* "Get me out of here!"

The two hornets hauled the irate mosquito up onto the dock leaf where he then lay panting, his wings muddy and crumpled and his nose just a little bent at the tip!

"Your nose is bent, Mr Mayor!" *said Horace, unwisely.*

"What did you say?" *screamed Squidge.*

"Er, I said 'you er now see this bee, ain't it', Mayor Squidge. Honest!"

"Did you now?" *replied the small insect squinting harshly at him.* "Well don't speak until you are spoken to. And what's this about a bee?"

Squidge looked more closely at Hermia, then jumped back. "It is a bee! A bee eh? Well, bee, what do you want then, he asked abruptly?" *hiding behind Wilger as he spoke.*

Wilger interrupted so as to get the credit: "I found her by the gorse bush, your honour. She is here on business, she says. She gave the password!"

"The password eh? Alright, bee. What kind of business is this and who sent you? Answer, or it will be the worse for you!"

Hermia didn't want to answer, but she was alarmed by the two large hornets and the ugly wasp, Wilger. She took her time so as to watch for a way to escape.

"I was given your name by a mutual friend," s*he replied innocently.* "He told me you could help me with an important matter."

"A fwend?" *snapped the mosquito.* "A fwend? Do I have any fwends, Wilger?" *Wilger sniggered.* "And who might this fwend be?"

"He told me his name was Fuddle. We discussed horses."

"Horses eh? That sounds like Fuddle." *And Squidge looked a little bit more more relaxed.* "Our Fuddle knows his stuff, he does – for a horsefly that is!" *He added with a touch of scorn.* "All right, so why, I wonder, did Fuddle send you here? Was it to sell me a horse?" *The mosquito turned to his followers threw back his head and laughed. One-by-one, they all laughed obediently.*

While this was going on Hermia began to back off very slowly, but first she leaned forwards, so that the backward movement would seem just to be good manners. "I am sure, though, that this is far too insignificant for a gnat of such importance as yourself." *Said Hermia, looking around her.* "It is only a flower I am seeking. Nothing that would interest such a busy insect. So, if it is all right with you, I will just be on my way and not cause you any more trouble."

"Not so fast, dear bee!" *said Squidge in his silkiest voice.* "If my fwend, Fuddle, sent you then has he not a good reason? After all we are all fwends here, aren't we boys?"

Horace let out a loud guffaw. "Why are you laughing Horace?" *Asked Squidge menacingly.*

"Oh no, I was just – er – being happy with my – er fwends, Mr Squidge."

"That's right Horace. And now you and I are fwends too, dear bee, aren't we!" *He said slyly.*

Hermia noticed his bent nose and studied it. Squidge followed her gaze and went a little boss-eyed staring at the sight of his warped nose.

It was now or never. Hermia suddenly shot up in the air, catching her guards quite unawares.

"Eh?" *yelled Wilger.*

"Get 'er!" *shouted Squidge … but as it happened no-one had noticed a newcomer to the scene, a rather large bumble bee, who, seeing the plight of the smaller bee, swooped down across the hornets' flight path and forced them to crash into Wilger. She called to Hermia:* "Quick, follow me!"

The two bees sped off through a patch of bull rushes, underneath a weeping willow tree and soon, weaving and winding amongst the tall grasses, they lost their pursuers in the undergrowth. Bertha, for this was the bumble bee's name, laughed and burst into song:

> "Though I bumble
> I never fumble
> When I stumble on a gnat!
>
> For though he's humble,
> His humour will crumble
> If you rumble what he's at!"

And, chuckling to herself, she led Hermia to an old tree right on the edge of Tripping Wood. They flew straight into her home, where Hermia collapsed exhausted into a small acorn armchair. Bertha looked down at her, smiled and went off to make a pot of blackcurrant tea.

Hermia looked across gratefully at the large form of Bertha bustling away, then sank into the soft down of her little chair.

BOOK EIGHT

Bertha and The Clue!

Bertha, the bumble bee gives Hermia her first real clue as to where the Golden orchid grows!

If you have tea
With a friendly bumble bee
You may find her platter
Will make you much fatter
Than if she were a flea!

The way Bertha greeted Hermia persuaded the bee how used to company her new friend was … and so she relaxed in these attractive surroundings, relieved and glad to catch her breath after the chase.

Bertha

"My dear, you must be exhausted," *said Bertha, soothingly.* "Those spiteful creatures; they have no manners at all … no style you know. Just you stretch out, my darling and don't be afraid to ask for anything, will you now."

The large bee reminded Hermia of a dramatic actress with her grand manner, dressed now in a large yellow and brown flowing gown.

"What a lovely gown!" *remarked Hermia.*

"Oh, just something I threw on," *smiled the other.* "Actually, my dear, it was given to me by a friend who lived in a hole in the wall of an old props room in a theatre. Can you imagine, someone actually snipped it from a much larger piece of fur —so large it could have covered five of your beehives – then they just dropped it, just like that right in front of my friend's house. What do you think of that?"

"Amazing!" *exclaimed Hermia, noting the very small drawing room, decorated as it was with a profusion of tiny flowers. The dandelion curtains concealed a world of lilies and lace, of ticking time-pieces, of trinkets and of very small teapots.*

"But bumble bees, you know, are really supposed to be simple!" *she sighed.*

"Such a beautiful simplicity," *Hermia said.*

As Bertha bustled in her kitchen, Hermia's eyes wandered to a portrait on the wall.

"Who is that?"

"That, my dear, is my father—such a handsome man don't you think?"

"He certainly has noble proportions!" *Hermia remarked, politely.*

"He once also had a home of noble proportions too," *sighed Bertha sadly.* "But that was before ..." *and her voice trailed off as she stood, gazing out of the window.*

"Before?" *echoed Hermia.*

"Oh, it all happened a long time ago. The swamp was not always a swamp you see. Once it was a great lake and the gardens of a grand house. Neat lawns rolled elegantly down to the water's edge; flowers danced in the wind to the music of the four seasons: shuddering in Winter; leaping and dancing in Spring; sprawling in Summer; moved only by occasional gusts and turning to pure gold and to flight in Autumn." *And she began to murmur:*

"Tis of Autumn's blush I'm singing
Who, blind and young awhile,
Does pluck a leaf then gild its grief
That none should think him vile.

Till Winter's eye comes gleaming,
His cousin's wealth to see
And battles fierce and glorious
Are fought with pagan glee.

Then Spring, bright child of God's good grace
Who, stronger still by half,
Stands bold and brash – his smile to flash -
The prodigal home at last.

Good fat Summer just sighs and spreads,
To gaze at wonders told.
He wines and dines, in warmth and smiles,
Till flowers sleep and leaves turn, once more, to gold.

Hermia realised the story was not going to come easily as she watched a small tear trickle down Bertha's cheek. But, then, Bertha blew her nose loudly and continued:

"The gardens were so full of flowers, my darling, that we never needed to go beyond them for food. My father told me the owner was such a keen gardener that he travelled the world simply to fill his greenhouses with wonderful flowers, you know sunflowers, roses, orchids ..."

"Stop!" *shouted Hermia.* "Did you say orchids?"

"Orchids? Oh yes, my dear, he simply loved orchids. Yes, as I was saying the great drive ran East, towards the house you see and was lined with huge poplar trees ..."

"Whoopee!" *yelled Hermia, tingling with excitement.*

"I beg your pardon?" *retorted Bertha, mildly upset at having been disturbed in her memories.*

But Hermia was by now flying around the room in a state of near hysteria. "You said 'orchids'! Bertha, you said 'orchids'!" *she cried.*

"Do be careful my dear," *said Bertha, concerned now both for her friend and for her ornaments. Finally, completely overwhelmed by the small bee's careless display of aeronautics, Bertha commanded:* "HERMIA SIT DOWN! WHAT IS THIS ALL ABOUT?"

Hermia laughed, sat down and looked at Bertha with sparkling eyes.

"Bertha, dear Bertha, I have travelled so far on a journey … a mission … a Royal Mission to discover a very special flower, one that is told in the myths and legends of our hive. In fact, Bertha, this flower is so special we all thought it was just a myth. And you, dear friend, have just told me where it will be – if it does exist still, she added cautiously!"

"I have?" *asked Bertha.* "How nice—I mean how very nice. But you see I only know that the greenhouse did exist, not that it does exist and I am afraid I cannot even tell you its exact position in the old garden – or swamp as it now is!" *she added sadly.* "Indeed, there is only one insect who would know and he is …"

"The Wise Green Dragonfly?" *asked Hermia brightly.*

"But that is right, my dear!" *said Bertha.*

Quest for the Golden Orchid

BOOK NINE

The Four Young Bees!

Appearances can deceive. This insect definitely looks like a dragonfly...

Damselfly

Truth is not dressed in finer clothes
But falsehood may wear silk down to its toes.
If you wish to be sure
Then listen for more:
For the simple truths (*that everyone knows*)!

Hermia flew back and forth, in the area between Tripping Wood and the swamp, in search of Ho, the Wise Green Dragonfly. She flew with the precision of a gardener mowing a bowling green, but the dragonfly was nowhere to be seen. Back and forth she went in straight-as-straight beelines, up and down, criss-crossing from one end to another-but there was no dragonfly! "Oh!" she complained crossly. But it made not the slightest bit of difference. "I think ..." she exclaimed, finally, stamping her feet ... "that the horsefly was right, after all. Dragonflies are obviously whimsical and disorganised creatures who do not know themselves where they are going! Oh!"

At this moment, a rather fine creature, with long lace-like wings, flew right up to Hermia.

And this creature was, to anyone's mind, certainly rather elegant.

"H-e-llo," *it said in a silky voice.* "Am I to understand, my dear, that you are looking for something valuable and that you need – ahem – a dragonfly to help you?"

"Oh!" *exclaimed Hermia, again.* "Oh yes … yes indeed. You might be..."

"My dear there is simply no 'might' about it. I am certainly the one you should be telling about this." *And the insect began to clean her wings with long strokes while watching Hermia closely.*

"Professor Dazzle and Bertha told me…they told me that Ho … that er, you would be able to tell me where the Golden Orchid was!"

"Did you say 'Golden' my dear … as in … gold?"

"Well yes, I suppose it must be gold if it is a Golden orchid. Don't you think?"

"Oh yes, rather," *she simpered.* "Where do you suppose one could wear it?"

Hermia looked strangely at the creature. "I hope you won't be offended if I observe that, for a Wise Green Dragonfly, you are not very green!" *she said.*

"Green, did you say?" *the insect murmured,* "Why would I need to be green?"

"I didn't suppose you need to be green if you aren't green," *Hermia replied, beginning to get confused again,* "but Ho is said to be green."

"Dear Ho. He sometimes gets lost, you know. I am not exactly Ho, you understand."

"Not exactly?"

"No, not exactly. You might if you looked at me carefully consider me to be his ... secretary?"

"Which is a very strange way of saying you are if you were, and not exactly saying you are not if you aren't!" *said Hermia, with a strong note of suspicion in her voice.*

"Do you know Fuddle, by any chance?" *she added.*

"Fuddle? That terrible horsefly? Of course, I don't know him," *the insect said indignantly.*

"Oh, you do know he is a horsefly, then?" *smiled Hermia, beginning to sense another trap.*

"Well, doesn't everyone, my dear? When I say I don't know him, I do mean socially, of course."

If Hermia had known better, she would have immediately recognised, not a dragonfly, wise or 'otherwise' but a Damselfly. (They are rather similar unless you know the difference.)

Hermia was just wondering what to do next when, instinctively, her nostrils quivered and her back straightened. She lifted her head and breathed in deeply. There was no doubt about it...none at all, "Honey!" *she cried,* "Honey! Sorry, but I must go!"

As the delightful scent overcame her, the bee began to forget everything. Her longing to see a hive again was just too strong. Without realising it, she lifted into the air and sailed into the aroma. As the powerful smell of honey grew stronger and stronger, Hermia moved faster and faster until, seeing in the distance a cherry tree, she could at last make out the hive hanging delicately in its branches.

"Well really!" exclaimed the Damselfly. "Some people have no manners." and, flicking her wings flew off in the opposite direction complaining loudly about the manners of bees and their complete lack of breeding!

As she drifted towards the hive, Hermia began to feel very homesick. Pictures of her old friends Hermione, Hyacinth, Dudley and Harmony came flooding back, and all she wanted was to be amongst bees again, to be in the company of a hive. Then, even above the wildly beating of her heart, she heard a frenzy of buzzing! Casting aside her first instinct to ignore the trouble; to carry on and reach the hive in safety, Hermia recalled Bertha's bravery in saving her own life. She leapt, with determination, towards the fight. So swiftly she moved, as both courage and fear drove her on.

A wasp, like a burglar attired,
By trouble would seem to be fired.
But it's chocolates and sweets
And sugary treats
That, by the wasp, are truly desired!

When in battle flight a warrior bee moves like an arrow, swift and sure. Just for a moment, the fight stopped as the adversaries listened to the high-pitched whine of the bee's flight. Her body was streamlined, her wings trimmed and she was in full fighting shape as she arrived at the source of the dispute.

In an instant, Hermia realised what was happening: four young bees, having been drawn to a picnic site, had been challenged over a drop of jam by a wasp but not any wasp. This was Wilger. Big and ugly as he was he easily outmatched the smaller bees. Hermia's whiskers trembled as she recognised her enemy.

Lowering her head and increasing her speed, she did not hesitate but shot into the middle of the group. Heedless of the danger, she knocked Wilger out of the sky.

The wasp, bewildered and blind with anger, banked around the tree, which *was above them and made a run through the branches to catch Hermia unawares. But, unknown to him, Hermia had continued her flight up, swooping to the top of the tree. As Wilger appeared from the middle of the tree the bee dropped like a stone and clipped the old wasp on the nose, bowling him over completely. Smarting from his defeat, Wilger had just enough breath to shout:*

"I'll get you for this, bee. That's twice that is," *and he flapped away angrily back to his gorse bush.*

Hermia began to feel drowsy. Sharp outlines now seemed mere vague and shapeless forms. Dulled with pain, she found herself being guided gently away. She did not even notice the four young bees drawing her into the hive. She was dreaming that she was building cells in the old apple tree again – one side, two sides, three sides, f-o-u-r ... until she fell into a deep and dreamless sleep.

BOOK TEN

Ho, The Wise Green Dragonfly!

*At last, Hermia meets Ho the Wise Green Dragonfly and
the search for the Golden Orchid begins in earnest!*

A dragonfly
Never flies very high
And won't even bother to hide.
His eyesight is such
That he doesn't have much
To fear on the average glide.

He'll swoop and he'll hover
From one place to another
With such perfect dignity and pride,
That the average frog,
As he sits on a log,
Will rarely catch him off-side!

*"So you are Hermia, are you?" The elegant musical voice seemed to tinkle like
a tiny bell. It enchanted her as she lay there basking in the early morning sunlight.
Hermia turned around, startled – was she still dreaming? She knew she*

had been led to the pond to get some sunshine and that had sounded like a voice, but no, seeing no-one, she nervously adjusted her position and decided: "I must be feverish. I was sure I heard a voice but there is no-one there!" *She settled back, stiffly, on her leaf. The bee was soon lulled once more in the morning haze; she watched the drifting leaves eddy in the breeze; the sun made her drowsy.* "You don't look anything like I imagined -" *the voice continued,* "- you really are very much smaller!"

"What? Who is that?" *Hermia asked, her eyes scanning the edge of the pond where the light danced teasingly upon the ripples, but all she could see was the odd pond hopper, an old frog who blinked at her apparently chewing his tongue and a cricket, who didn't seem intelligent enough to even pass the time of day. A small whirlpool appeared from the gulp of a fish.*

"Good morning, how are you feeling now?" *piped a small voice from beside her.*

"Is that you Fizzy?" *asked Hermia, recognising one of the younger bees who had taken her into the hive two days earlier.* "Was that you saying those things just now?"

"What things?"

"Oh … nothing. Never mind. I thought I heard someone say something."

"I came to see if you would like a cupful of honey."

"That's very thoughtful of you," *said Hermia,* "but I notice your combs are not very full just now. Why is that?"

"That is true!" *sighed Fizzy.* "Somehow we have not been lucky with the pollen this year. The wiser bees say it is the fault of the metal creatures which spray the land with poison. They say things are not as they should be and so our combs are empty. But," *she added,* "we are not so poor that we cannot share what we do have!"

Impressed, Hermia simply stared at the pool. Then, as if she were dreaming she caught sight of a reflection.

It was a long thin body with gossamer wings which, fanning the water, stirred up small ripples over the smooth surface. Hermia looked up quickly and there, right behind her, was the smiling face of Ho, The Wise Green Dragonfly.

"Oh!" *gasped Hermia.*

"Hello," *replied Ho.*

The two studied each other for what seemed to Hermia an age.

"I understand you have been looking for me."

"Yes!" *was all Hermia could reply.*

"Well?" *laughed Ho.* "Now you've found me."

Hermia burst into tears of relief while Ho just glided up into the air and hovered awhile before lightly settling on a leaf.

"Fizzy, although it is unusual for a dragonfly to eat honey, I would dearly like to sample some," *he said.* "Would you be kind enough to fetch me a small morsel?"

"Oh yes sir, certainly sir," *replied Fizzy glad to be of help, particularly to someone so highly respected, and she rushed off to get some.*

Ho preened his wings for a moment and waited until Hermia was ready to speak.

Smiling through her tears, Hermia said simply,

"I'm so pleased to meet you."

"Bertha has spoken very highly of you," *replied Ho.* "She tells me you are searching for something; something of value for your hive and that I may be of help to you."

"Oh yes, yes indeed. Dear Bertha … she says … she says you know where the Golden Orchids grow!"

"We may be jumping ahead here. I know, from tradition, that there was what was called a greenhouse – a glistening glass house with five sides and in this house orchids once grew. I know from tales where this stood, which I suppose is a start."

"Five sides? Did you say FIVE sides?" *Hermia almost yelled, trembling a little from a memory way from Apple Tree Hive in, what seemed, an age ago.*

"Yes, five sides. Its back was against an old wall which had a door in it. So it had three sides around it and two on top. Alas, it fell into disuse and it fell apart. It stands no longer in the centre of the garden, where once the sunlight shone through its windows and the gardener toiled within its frame to produce good and wonderful plants. It is not now as it was then,

54

of course. Who knows if any of the orchids still grow, or if they have all died off!"

"But the legend has not died, Ho," *Hermia reminded him, smiling warmly at his gentle manners.* "Can a legend live except there be some truth in it?"

"Some legends are exaggerated, you know, or changed to make a good story," *he said. Then he seemed to go into a trance as he repeated words which he had heard long ago:*

Words were warriors once
And in the company of truth were seen.
(While others are acrobats performing stunts
From tongues too keen.)

"I beg your pardon?" *asked Hermia.*

"A wise old Praying Mantis told me these words a long time ago and your words reminded me of them," *smiled Ho.* "It's nothing, nothing at all."

At that moment, Fizzy returned with the honey and gave it to Ho who sipped it gratefully.

Hermia sighed, "Strangely, your words comfort me, dear Ho. I feel stronger already."

"Then you must tell me what you want of me," *he said, simply,* "and I shall then tell you if I believe I can be of assistance."

"Will you show me where the greenhouse stood?"

"Gladly," *replied Ho,* "but do not expect it to be easy!"

It was Hermia's turn to pause.

"There must be complete silence," *continued the dragonfly,* "because there will be danger and we must neither make ourselves a target nor swerve from our intention. But first we must pay attention to details and then we should find what we are looking for!"

"Hooray!" *cheered Fizzy, who had been hanging on every word.* "Can I come too?"

Ho looked across at the small bee and appeared to be thinking. Finally, he spoke.

"I do believe you can."

"What about us?" *came three small voices from behind the bush,* "Can we come too?"

"Zipper, Whizzer and Twizzle what are you doing eavesdropping on our private talk?" *rebuked Hermia, mildly.*

"Oh, we were only listening," *answered Twizzle for the other two, who looked a little embarrassed at being discovered.*

"You see what I mean about silence," *laughed Ho.* "Come along then. We must waste no more time." *And off they flew - Hermia to her destiny, the others to adventure.*

Quest for the Golden Orchid
BOOK ELEVEN

Into the Swamp!

The bees and Ho reach the centre of the swamp to find all is not quiet there!

Where, you may ask, do orchids grow;
Are they cloistered in soil that is sieved?
If you are careful to look
By a babbling brook
You may find where such delicacy lives.

It's not in a vase,
Nor behind plate glass,
That you'll find this beauty awhile.
Such flowers are rare
But grow, without care,
On a tip; on a heap; on a pile.

Into the swamp flew the six. Though where they were heading Hermia had no idea. She followed the dragonfly, obediently, confident in the company of this sparkling being. The others also seemed quite at ease. Swooping low over bushes, through brambles and branches, the five bees and Ho reached the first signs of the swamp. Bulrushes stood like soldiers at attention, the reeds trembling in the breeze. However, as they worked deeper and deeper into the swamp, the branches arched ... the brambles snatched. The sweet scent of meadow grass gave way to the marshy and cloying stench of the bog. It began to be stifling. Yet Ho seemed to know exactly where he was going. Without hesitation, he led them ever further into the terror of the swamp, into the dark, damp and airless wastes.

Hermia was curious to know where the old greenhouse had stood and, were it not for the threat of Wilger and his cronies, she would have asked. But, as the silence closed in around them, no-one spoke a word.

Ho began to slow down, signalling to the others to do the same. Hermia looked up and was almost blinded by a shaft of light which seemed to spread a golden carpet across the clearing ahead.

"This looks familiar," *murmured Hermia, very quietly, looking around her.*

"I'm not surprised," *answered Ho, landing lightly on a thistle.* "Bertha told me the tale, but look over there," *he whispered, and as the ground mist cleared, the bees saw what Ho was pointing at.*

There, right in front of them, squirming, squatting and plotting, was a vast array of what seemed, at first sight, to be all the worst kinds of insect one could imagine. And they were apparently listening to a speaker!

"Here?" *gasped Hermia.*

"Exactly," *smiled Ho,* "the very place!"

The Dock Leaf, Little Nettles, The Swamp, looked a very different place from when Hermia had escaped the clutches of Horentious Squidge only a few days before. Instead of seeing a small creature trembling beneath a leaf, there now stood that same mosquito, balanced proudly upon a sunflower, his thin whining voice whistling across the clearing.

"Doesn't he know that there is perhaps the finest collection of orchids beneath his stinging nettles?" *asked Hermia.*

"He is only interested in the 'finest' collection of rogues in front of him!" *sighed Ho.*

"Shall we rush them, Ho?" *asked Whizzer, his whiskers trembling with excitement.*

Hermia looked fondly at him, "Silly!" *she said.*

As the mist cleared a little more, Whizzer saw the extent of Squidge's power. There were more than a thousand wasps and a band of hornets immediately around him!

"They certainly wouldn't notice one more wasp ..." *murmured Zipper with a chuckle.*

Hermia looked curiously at the small bee, and then, with a sudden flash of insight, laughed with him. "You are absolutely right, Zipper and how very clever."

It was Ho's turn to be puzzled. "Well, you two, come along spill the beans. What are you plotting?"

"It is really a simple childish plan that should work, Ho," *smiled Hermia.*

"When we were small ..." *began Fizzy,* "we would all find a large flower filled with pollen ..." *interrupted Twizzle,* "And then ..." *continued Whizzer,* "We would be bright yellow you see ..." *shouted Zipper, as quietly as he could.* "And so would look just like wasps," *finished Hermia with a laugh, remembering fondly the games of bees and wasps she also used to play as a youngster.*

"The last time I saw Zipper in the company of a wasp," *said Whizzer, scornfully,* "he was flapping around like a butterfly with a stomach ache."

Zipper looked a little hurt but soon brightened up when Ho said "Do you know it just might work, Zipper. Well done! Hermia, do you feel up to it?"

"Oh, I want to go. It was my idea," *complained Zipper, rather too loudly.*

"Hush, Zipper," *whispered Hermia,* "you know it is my Quest, and so, brave as you are, it is I who must go."

Impetuous as ever, Hermia, without a second thought dived down towards a patch of clover. Without further ado, she began to roll in it. First she rolled one way; then she rolled the other. Then she sneezed violently, scattering a host of tiny midges who all twittered, "Funny bee, funny bee," *and danced even more excitedly.*

"Haven't you ever seen a bee taking a pollen bath before?" *she asked mustering as much dignity as she could.*

"Tee hee, tee hee, tee hee," *was the only reply she got from the silly insects.*

Hermia flew back to the others. "Oh Hermia, you do look funny," *laughed Twizzle.*

"But will it fool them do you think?" *asked Ho?*

"Oh, if we brush some off in lines here and … there," *said Fizzy drawing a feeler around Hermia.*

"That's better," *said Twizzle.*

Hermia wiped her own feelers through her lips, took a deep breath and glided silently into the midst of the mob. Ho instructed the younger bees to return to warn the hive that something was amiss. But, as he turned to watch them go, he noticed Zipper slipping down to the pollen patch which Hermia had left just a few moments before.

Quest for the Golden Orchid

BOOK TWELVE

The Gnat's Plot!

The gnat begins to persuade the other insects to attack the hive!

The snail, it crawls so ever-so-slow,
So ever-so ever-so-slow!
So that, if you catch
It on a cabbage patch,
You may possibly, probably, know,
That when it begins, you
May be sure, it continues
To arrive where it intended to go -
To go.
To arrive where it intended to go!

Its progress is such,
That it's not overmuch -
No, it's not too much bothered with speed.
If it doesn't arrive
Before half past five
It will sit in its shell and snort, 'blow!'
'Oh, blow!'

It will sit in its shell and snort, 'blow!'
Oh, a snail it crawls so ever-so, ever-so,
ever-so ever-so …
S-L-O-W!

Squidge stood gazing nobly about him. That is to say, Squidge intended to gaze nobly about him.

However, an experienced observer might have noticed that, above the spindly legs, the large bandage that was tied around his snout made his already narrow appearance seem a little too comic … or that his chin jutted out just that little bit too far.

Apart from this, however, anyone not knowing he was just a malicious little gnat might have mistaken him for an actor in the heroic mould, testing the boards before making his entrance. To make matters worse, Squidge had caught a cold falling into the mud, so that every time he shouted it sounded like the whistle of a bosun on a ship announcing the arrival of the captain on board.

"Fwends, *(sniff)*" *he squeeked,* "for many years now it has always been the bees who have taken all the honey … *(sniff)*!"

"Shame … shame!" *yelled the mob, in approval.*

"Yes, dear fwends, time and again they have stolen it from us poor … *(sniff)* … starving … *(squeak)* … hard working creatures!"

"Hooray, hear-hear," *went the crowd, a little uncertainly because somehow they felt that something was not quite right about this; it jangled in their heads! But, on the other hand, it did sound promising!*

Squidge looked around, rather pleased with the effect he was having on his audience.

"That's it, fwends: they have stolen – yes - stolen the honey from us poor hard working and caring creatures who … *(squeak)* … labour day and night just to have a good time – I mean … *(sniff - squeak)* … who labour to make ends meet."

At these almost well-chosen words, the crowd went wild; so much so that a caterpillar fell off a dock leaf in his enthusiasm. (Or perhaps he had just eaten through it!)

Squidge smiled broadly. He now had them in the palm of his hand. "Let it not be said," *he added slyly,* "that your beloved Mayor Squidge would allow his fwends to starve … *(sniff)* … and be ruled by these 'agwessive' and dangerous creatures … a-a-a-tissuuuueeee!

"Bravo, bravo!" *shouted the heaving mass of insects below.*

"And" … *continued the mosquito looking about him cunningly …* "I have it on the best authority that, at this very moment, these cruel monsters are planning to attack us in the very heart of our … *(squeak)* … beloved swamp!"

While Squidge's audience expressed various depths of horror and outrage at this statement, Hermia smiled, aware that Squidge did not yet know how near the truth he was.

The mosquito was now in full voice and it rose to a tremendous squeak as he uttered the words: "But I, dear fwends, I, Horentious Marcus Alphonso Squidge, respected mayor of this brave little community will, without fear for my own safety, lead you to the victory you deserve!"

The din was overpowering as Squidge bowed and scraped, to the delight of the mob. Then, as he prepared to outline his plan, Hermia climbed on top of a snail to be able to hear better.

"Listen to that nice mosquito, Arthur. What is he saying now?" *said the snail.*

Snails

"He is tellin' us, Mildred, that the bees are goin' to give us some of their honey if we ask them nicely – Ah think!"

"Well isn't that just kind of them, and what a good mayor to organise this," *said Mildred.* "It will certainly be a change from cabbage leaves, won't it, Arthur!"

"There's nowt wrong wi' cabbage leaves!" *replied Arthur, rather upset by his wife's comments.* "Why, I have been eating cabbage leaves, snail and boy since, well since I was quite young, and I have to say I am rather partial to cabbage leaves Mildred."

At this, the snail humped himself down in his shell and didn't come out for a week, it is said. Unfortunately, however, this unseated Hermia who had just leant forward to hear the finish of the plan. She slipped off the snail onto a gangly looking harvester who rebuked her soundly, wagging one thin leg while peering through his small spectacles.

"Kindly behave yourself, young lady," *he said in a dithering kind of voice,* "some of us are trying to listen to a … hmmm … very interesting debate on the local availability of honey and the … hmmm … er, previous historical … er.. significance of bees in relation to … er … this. If people insist on falling on you from every angle every few minutes, it is going to be very difficult to hear the speaker, who is a very … hmmm … well known mosquito, I am led to believe." *At this, his spectacles fell off his nose.*

The disturbance, unfortunately, had caught the attention of a wasp, a rather large wasp with a scarred face and a patch over one eye. He was studying Hermia very closely through this one fierce eye. Oh yes, without a doubt this was Wilger, Hermia's arch enemy and, without a doubt he was beginning to suspect something.

Hermia began to move calmly through the crowd and away from the wasp, but she felt the puzzling eye of her enemy following her with an unblinking stare … until …

recognition lit the eye and Wilger let out a terrific roar:

"It's that bee. Stop her she's a spy!"

Hermia darted into the startled crowd and pushed her way forwards. She was trembling in fear. Then, suddenly, without warning, she felt herself held fast in the arms of a small bright yellow wasp with sparkling eyes.

"Oh no," *wailed Hermia,* "I shall never escape now!"

"I told you it was my idea," *whispered the wasp.*

"Zipper, is that you?" *gasped Hermia.*

"Good isn't it – the disguise I mean," *spluttered Zipper, trying not to laugh.*

"No time to waste. I'll confuse them while you make a break for it. Don't worry about me. I won't get caught."

"All right, but take care," *cried Hermia, as she took off under an overhanging branch and Zipper, thoroughly enjoying himself, first prodded two fat hornets, whose battle he did not wait to watch, tripped up a centipede and flew straight through the tight formation of wasps which now were in hot pursuit of Hermia, yelling:* "Oh sorry, terribly sorry, whoops, are you all right there, my fault, my fault, so sorry ..." *and confusion reigned.*

Quest for the Golden Orchid

BOOK THIRTEEN

Hermia's Flight!

Hermia escapes and thinks up a plan to outwit Squidge!

If, when in flight
You feel the dark night of despair
Your heart surround,
Remember this – though help seems far -
That life and love abound.

A whirling and twirling of insects surrounded Hermia as she made her escape from her enemies in the nettle patch. Behind her, in the distance, she could just hear Squidge, in his sunflower, screaming: "Get that bee, get that bee!"

Beneath him, perched in the leaves was a nest of young earwigs who became startled by the thumping from above as Squidge stamped his little feet in fury. Wiggly nipped Waggly - who then nipped Wugly -

Earwig

Earwig

-who ran down the stem of the sunflower and through the legs of an old harvester - who clipped a wasp with his walking stick - who tried to sting a beetle - who bumped into Lilly the Ladybird - who ran up the sunflower …

One minute Squidge was standing there, master of all he surveyed. The next minute he was turning a neat and helpless circle in front of the whole assembly. Then, disappearing into the undergrowth on the back of a huge stag beetle which suddenly raced away at great speed, Squidge's thin squeaky voice could be heard shouting: "Dead or alive!"

Deeper and deeper into the swamp flew Hermia. Aware that they were all in danger, she led her pursuers away from Ho and the others. "If only Bertha had told me more about the swamp I would know which way to go now," *she thought. Hermia was generally happier flying in straight lines and with a plan, but there was no time to make a plan. She was being pursued by a host of hostile hornets.* "Oh, what tall trees!" *she thought as a row of huge Poplar trees loomed up all in a line.* "Such tall trees … …!

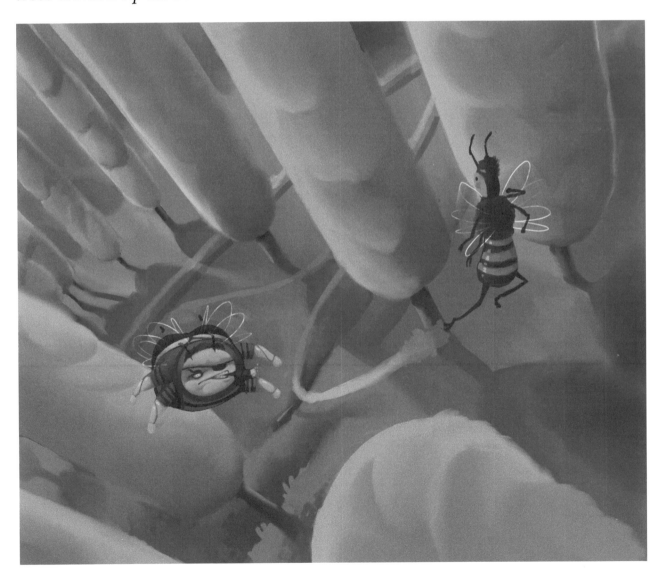

Just a minute, wasn't there something Bertha mentioned about an avenue of Poplars … which lined a road eastwards towards the house? I have it," *she yelled, and then more quietly to herself:* "If I follow the line of trees they will have the sun in their eyes. They will expect me to fly in a straight line, as bees do."

Hermia could almost smell Wilger as he fought to gain on her. Without a second thought, she turned into the avenue of trees. One minute, Wilger had her in his sights. The next …?

The spiral and twist which the bee performed in that split second was stunning. One minute she was there … the next there was empty space. The movement was so swift that she lost all her pursuers … except one.

Cunning old Wilger had followed her and was right behind her … His superior strength was beginning to triumph.

Hermia, gasping for breath said a prayer. It seemed as if there was no hope. She looked desperately around for help …

A glimmer caught her attention … It wasn't only the shaft of light which lit up the hole in the trunk of the tree ahead of her, but also the shining pair of eyes looking through the hole which made her look more closely. Hermia made an inspired guess and headed straight for the hole. She folded her wings tightly at the last minute and shot through. Once the other side, Ho, whose eyes they were, encouraged Hermia to keep going, but it was too much to resist looking back to see Wilger, poor fat Wilger glowering, stuck firmly in the hole.

One hour later, Ho and Hermia sat, motionless, listening to Zipper as he outlined the plot that Squidge was hatching against the hive. The cunning insect meant to draw out the bees, and trap them in an old tree trunk!

Hermia began to dream once more while watching the clouds drift lazily across the sky. It was as if the wind rustled … 'Hush-hush' … in Hermia's mind. She seemed to be moving into the great breath of nature … 'no rush, no rush,' … whispered the tree tops. She was drawn into the gentle rhythms … the wind rocked her as in a boat which sailed in a sea of dreams. Lapping upon her senses, they began to take on the many colours of the rainbow …when, suddenly, she awoke from her trance, muttering:

"Woodlice!"

Ho turned towards Hermia. "I beg your pardon?"

"Oh, woodlice," *repeated Hermia,* "they chew wood you know."

"That is indeed so," *he said kindly,* "and?"

"Yes, but you see," *insisted Hermia,* "Professor Dazzle studies them. He is a brilliant moth, and he told me that they chew wood. They chew it up into little pieces. They go in one side and come out the other."

"Are you feeling all right, my dear?" *asked the dragonfly.*

"Never felt better," *replied Hermia heartily,* "and butterflies."

At that, Ho threw up his hands in despair and spoke to Zipper:

"Go and fetch Hermia some water, Zipper. I think it must be all the excitement."

"No, listen to me both of you. We need to know where the trap is to be laid, so we need some butterflies who can fly slowly and listen to the plan in more detail as they are passing. They can then guide the woodlice to a particular spot to help us. Ho, you must go and warn the hive. Zipper, you must fetch Whizzer, Fizzy and Twizzle, and then we must search for Admiral Brisk and Professor Dazzle. Tell the hive to act as if they know nothing, but to pretend to fall into the trap. Then we shall release them from the trap to spring such a surprise on Squidge. We must let him believe he is winning!"

Ho nodded wisely. "I believe you have a plan, after all and it is true that the branch that bends in the wind does not break!"

Quest for the Golden Orchid

BOOK FOURTEEN

The Battle for Cherry Tree Hive!

At the edge of the clearing, five thousand pairs of eyes gleamed. Five thousand bodies, humming and strumming the song of battle, were poised. The wasps were waiting for the signal to attack.

Meanwhile, the small hive, which hung in the old cherry tree near the swamp, seemed only to be dreaming. It dreamed as if there was really nothing to worry about on such a beautiful day. Of course, it might seem rather too still for an intelligent eye, but not so to a greedy and impatient wasp.

Seemingly unconcerned, across the clearing, a single bee flew. The eyes which followed the flight moved as one. The bees, meanwhile, waited, balanced upon the branch of a fallen tree, not a wing out of place.

The silence seemed almost stifling. Some instinct sent more sensitive creatures into hiding. The wasp felt sure that no-one had seen the intruders arrive … no one that is except, perhaps one harmless-looking dragonfly who darted in front of their very eyes. But then dragonflies do, don't they?

The stillness seemed to creep across the long grasses towards the hive and then shuddered … but that was just the wind … wasn't it?

The large wasp watched, then moved stiffly. A blackbird broke from the bushes uttering its staccato cry of warning, but still the hive seemed to take no notice. Wilger had a moment of suspicion. He scanned the clearing slowly from one side to the other. As he did so, ten thousand pairs of eyes closed simultaneously and nothing betrayed the presence of the bees on the other side of the clearing, except, perhaps, the hum of their wings as, occasionally they beat to keep balance.

'That is just the wind,' thought Wilger, as he fought to control the anger he could feel bristling up inside him after his last brush with Hermia.

The wasp was nervous and almost hesitated, but the tension of the group was mounting as their bodies strained forwards.

Wilger paused as he went over the plan once more in his burly head: 'Draw the bees out away from the hive!' That was what he had to do. But what if they already knew the plan? What if they had laid a trap for him? What if …? But as he caught the eyes of the others around him he knew it was too late to be wondering and, suddenly, without a sign, the five thousand wasps threw themselves into the attack.

"This is a bit more like it, eh Drizzle? A butterfly of action, that's me. None of that namby-pamby stuff amongst the roses for me, old moth – eh? What d'ye say, doesn't it make the old wings un-crinkle? Mind you it could be the effects of the --- er, well never mind."

"My name, Admiral is Dazzle. Excitement and suspense are, of course, studies all of their own and should be handled carefully. Vould you not agree, Admiral?"

"Oh absolutely, without a doubt; hit the nail on the head there, Drizzle old chap.

No trouble for its own sake, eh! You boffins have got something in those heads of yours. No wonder you all go bald, eh? Too much for the old noddle and not enough nourishment for the hair, old chap. Now if you were to take a nip of this little something I have here, three times a day – well I can only say, even if you did stay bald, you wouldn't care either way!"

"Sank you, Admiral, but I sink ve haf work to do now."

"Oh quite, definitely; get the little so and sos on parade and don't let them break ranks until we arrive. Got it? A forced march, that's the thing." Meanwhile, my chaps are doing a few balmy sorties over the enemy's heads. Whoops! Did you see that one? Old Charlie is a bit hazy on his downwind runs. I'll have to give him a few pointers."

"Yes ... now, if you vill excuse me, Admiral, I am not so happy in the light and I must do my duty. Goodbye."

Oh yes, absolutely old chap. Chin up. See you by the tree trunks. Tally ho!"

In a bush, at the head of a guard of six thousand bees, Hermia felt her blood pounding. She watched, knowing that, at any minute, four cohorts of bees with her friends Zipper, Whizzer, Twizzle and Fizzy in charge would leap out to attack the wasps and then follow them into the trap.
Then, in the middle of the clearing, three lines of wasps, attacking wildly, met the first line of bees …….. and the battle for Cherry Tree Hive had begun.

Zzzzzzzzzzz

zzzzzzzzzzzzzzzz

zzzzzzzzzzzzzzzzz

zzzzzzzzzzzzzzzzzzzzzzp

went the bees, leaping boldly into the attack.

The wasps turned so neatly, so very neatly. (The planning was very clear to the bees now.) The wasps circled twice and then fled, leading the bees - off and away ………… far into the swamp!
Hermia bit her lip. She could do nothing now but wait for the plan to unfold. For at this moment she had no idea what Squidge's next move would be! Squidge did not disappoint them. He treated his prey to a display which was quite unexpected.
At that moment, and, as if covering the sky above them, a whole host of hornets appeared over the hive. This was a threat no-one had foreseen!

While this was happening, deeper and deeper into the swamp dashed the four cohorts of bees. They pursued the wasps relentlessly, as they had been told to do.

All of a sudden, the four flights of wasps wheeled high into the air and, as if scattering, dived into four hollow tree trunks. Through four small entrances they dived, followed closely by the bees. (This, of course, was a revenge thought up by Wilger for his earlier disgrace of being stuck in the hole of the tree when he had chased Hermia!)

As soon as the wasps entered they began leaving immediately through a small hole low down in the stump of the tree. While this was happening and so soon as the bees had all entered the tree a spider criss-crossed the hole with his sticky web. Then, as the last wasp left the tree stump at the bottom, so the same trick was carried out over the other hole – leaving the bees locked inside! There seemed no way out!

As the wasps flew back confidently and in deadly formation towards the hive, sixteen thousand of the hive's best bees were now left trapped in the trees, unable to defend it. How could Hermia now defend the hive?

Back at the hive all could see that the sky was filled with hornets! There was no way to save the hive unless Hermia could at least free the bees from their prison? She watched in horror as wasp after wasp entered the unprotected hive. She was just about to fling her ten thousand bees into a reckless attack, when she saw Ho, waving frantically.

Meanwhile, deep inside the tree stump, the four young bees were trying to make themselves heard.

"Hush, please," *pleaded Fizzy.*

"Oh, do be quiet!" *screamed Twizzle.*

"Shut up!" *Yelled Whizzer.*

"Listen!" *Bellowed Zipper.*

The older bees turned around, in amazement.

"By what right do you command here, young Zipper?" *demanded an elder.*

"I mean listen 'here' ..." *said Zipper more quietly* ... "down here!" *as he pointed somewhere into the mouldy dark of the tree stump.*

The bees then all stopped to listen. Their heads gradually turned downwards towards the tiny sound of chomping somewhere far below in the roots of the old tree.

"Woodlice, you see," *explained Zipper, triumphantly.* "Woodlice. They belong to Hermia. They are chewing a hole for us to escape, do you see?"

Back, near the hive an amazing scene was taking place. It seemed that the hornets were no longer a threatening force. They were being dispersed by a huge battalion of bumble bees led by the round and warlike figure of Bertha who appeared to be singing!

And within the tree trunk the bees did now 'see' because, at that moment, the first woodlice broke through, sending a small shower of fine dust into the chamber and, silently, the bees began to escape. Wasting no time, Hermia led her ten thousand bees into the hive. Here, a great battle was now taking place. The attacking wasps had caused chaos. Many were just gorging themselves on the precious supplies of honey. Others were attempting to carry it away. The bees, although hopelessly outnumbered, set about the wasps bravely, taking no thought for themselves but only for the good of the hive, which seemed doomed. Hermia, gashed and bleeding, cheered her bees on, when, to her immense relief, through the trees raced the rest of the bees, released at last from the tree trunk. The bees burst through the unguarded door of the hive. The first group, led by Zipper, let out a blood-curdling buzz; then the second, led by Whizzer was followed closely by the third group, with Twizzle racing to keep ahead and, finally, the fourth group, with Fizzy yelling and cheering in the lead, all soared high into the air.

On their own territory and descending on the wasps in a surprise attack they threw the shabby intruders into complete and utter disarray.

As the wasps fled, the bees let out a great cry of victory.

Hermia, looking around her caught sight of two dark and sorry figures limping off into the swamp. She recognised the bulky form of Wilger supporting the thin and weedy shape of Squidge, as they shuffled, broken, into the swamp.

Quest for the Golden Orchid
BOOK FIFTEEN
Peace Returns ...

The evening sun slanted through the trees and, while the insects flew lazily amongst the tall wildflowers which bordered the busy hive, a hum of celebration could be heard within.

The bees were repairing the combs and cells, bringing water to the hive and, though the supplies were few and far between, some pollen too. It seemed as if the dank and moist heaviness of the swamp which had hung for so long in the air about them was, somehow, disappearing.

As Hermia and Ho sat together enjoying the sunset, a familiar song seemed to be carried upon the breeze:

> "Though I bumble
> I never fumble
> When I stumble on a gnat!
>
> For though he's humble,
> His humour will crumble
> If you rumble what he's at!"

"That, if I am not mistaken," *said Ho, smiling,* "is the voice of our dear friend, Bertha, celebrating her part in our magnificent victory."

"I must say, Ho, that she appeared to leave that rather late!" *complained Hermia.* "It seemed to be raining hornets!"

"Bertha is a great friend and ally, but she will hurry for no-one," *he replied, laughing.*

"Oh, how about some tea?" *bellowed Bertha, as she alighted onto a slim branch nearby.* "I have some blackberry jam which, even though I say it myself, is rather good."

"Gracious lady, I would dearly like to accept, but I really must return to my pond," *replied Ho.* "There is so much to do there. However, I cannot speak for Hermia. In fact, looking at her, I am not sure she can speak for herself at the moment. She seems as if she is quite unable to make up her mind about … about something."

Hermia looked intently at Ho. "How could you know that Ho?" *she asked him.*

"It's as plain as the sting in your tail," *interrupted Bertha.* "You are as silent as a moth; your face is as long as a praying mantis and you are kicking your heels like a centipede. Now, what exactly is troubling you, my dear?"

Ho spoke for the bee: "Hermia doesn't know whether to stay or to go, poor bee," *he said gently, as a small tear ran down Hermia's cheek.*

"There, there," *murmured Bertha, kindly.* "Why don't you come and stay with me for a while? I do so enjoy company, you know."

Hermia smiled for the first time in what seemed an age, replying: "I would love to Bertha, but I have not finished my Quest, you see! I am commanded to return to Apple Tree Hive to take some of the pollen of the Golden Orchid for Queen Gertrude. Her Majesty is expecting me."

"That is right!" *said Ho, firmly.*

"But what of my friends here?" *wailed Hermia.* "They need me to help them find pollen for the Winter honey supply!" *She stared glumly into the swamp.* "What am I to do?" *she wept.*

"That is right, you must help them!" *Ho asserted.*

At this Hermia looked up at him with one eye. "Just a minute, Ho, I said I must return to Apple Tree Hive and you just said, 'That is right'"

"That is right," *affirmed Ho.*

"And then, when I said I wanted to help my friends here in Cherry Tree Hive, you also said, 'That is right'!"

"Yes, that is right," *affirmed Ho.*

"But you can't tell me to do both of these things. I thought you were supposed to be a WISE Green Dragonfly!"

"Yes … that is right," *repeated Ho, trying not to laugh.*

"Oh, do stop it, Ho," *cried Bertha.* "You are teasing the poor bee. Do tell her what you are thinking."

"Well," *began Ho,* "where there is night, soon there will be the day. Big does not exist without there is small. Warm and cool are opposites."

"BUT WHAT DOES ALL THIS MEAN, HO?" *begged Hermia.* "I don't understand."

"If these things are true," *answered Ho,* "then, where there is a problem there must also exist its opposite – a solution!"

"I am sure you are right dear Ho, but could you please tell me what it is?" *answered the bee, almost pleading with him.*

"Will you tell her, Bertha?" *implored Ho, unable to contain his laughter anymore.*

"You see, Hermia, it is really quite simple. As you say you must return with some of the pollen, therefore, so you must!"

"I really couldn't have put that better myself, Bertha," *laughed Ho, even louder.*

"But what about the …? Oh," *said Hermia, her face lighting up.* "You mean …?"

"Of course, you silly bee, the remaining pollen will be gathered by the bees and this will see them through the winter."

"Ohhh," *screamed Hermia.* "How clever you both are!"

"Hermia, just one thing ..." *said Bertha.* "Yes?"

"You have not yet actually found the Golden orchid! And another thing, did you see which way that gnat went?"

"Why?" *asked Hermia, wide-eyed.*

"Because, my dear, you must follow him … you must follow him to find the Golden Orchid … and besides, he owes me a garden," *replied Bertha with a very distant look.*

The two bees leapt as one into the air and flew, with reckless speed, after the gnat and the wasp. They flew past the long trailing branches of trees covered with ivy, over bushes and through long beds of waving reeds, deep into the old swamp. They overtook the cowering mosquito and his allies and headed straight for Dock Leaf Mansions, Little Nettles where Hermia had once seen Squidge hold court.

They paused.

"Are you sure it will be here, Bertha?" *asked Hermia, trembling.*

"We cannot be certain, Hermia," we must search and see!"

Hermia and Bertha then circled around and began from opposite directions. They looked high … they looked low but nowhere could they find an orchid of any sort, let alone a Golden Orchid.

"Oh dear," *gasped Hermia,* "There are no flowers here except Squidge's sunflower, some clover and a few dandelions!"

"I am so sorry, my dear," *Murmured the big bee.* "I was so sure your flower would be here. You are certain this IS where the old greenhouse stood?"

"This is just where Ho said it had been!" *wept Hermia.*

The two bees turned to go; Bertha to her house and Hermia, sadly, back to Queen Gertrude to tell her of her failure. She lifted, quietly (for a bee), into the air. But, just as she was turning to say goodbye, a huge buzzing sound could be heard getting nearer and nearer!

Bzzzzzzzzzzz*zzzzzzzzzzzzzZZZZZZZp*

Wilger, the ugly old wasp raced out from behind a tree. He hit Hermia sideways and knocked her to the ground. He flew up and around, mocking her and laughing cruelly, "Ha, ha, I got you that time bee. You can't get one over, lightly, on old Wilger!" *and, laughing still, he shot off back to his gorse bush on the edge of the swamp.*

Bertha rushed over to Hermia, but, to her amazement found that the small bee was also laughing, even louder than Wilger. "My dear," *she cried,* "are you quite alright? Did you bump your head? Are you hysterical? Shall I fetch some honey for you?"

"Oh do stop fussing, dear Bertha," *yelled Hermia,* "can't you see what I have found?"

Bertha looked more closely. She gasped. "Hermia, if that old wasp knew what he had done when he hit you he would be the sore one. Well, well, well," *she laughed,* you have found it ……. You have found the fabulous Golden Orchid!"

"No, I haven't, Bertha. I haven't found the Golden Orchid. I have found hundreds and hundreds of Golden Orchids!

Just look at them. They are hidden beneath this great tangle of weeds. Who would imagine that such a beautiful flower could grow in such surroundings?"

And sure enough she had found her treasure. The seeds must surely have drifted when the greenhouse rotted away. They had spread their wonderful blooms and grown like a flight of golden butterflies, but poised in still life.

Hermia didn't wait for Bertha to follow. She simply sped back to Cherry Tree Hive and, calling all the bees to follow her, led the triumphant band to the orchids which had grown underneath the huge old bush through which she had fallen. The bees, once their amazement was over, were very busy now; too busy to talk (which is perhaps why you don't hear bees talking much). They gathered as much pollen as they could carry to take back to the hive to make their precious honey for the winter.

Hermia, meanwhile, without saying anything to anyone took a great amount of pollen in the pollen sacks on her legs and set off, in a straight bee-line, but this time towards her first home, Apple Tree Hive; to her old friends. This didn't take nearly so long this time because now she knew the way. When she arrived, Desmond happened to be right there, in the entrance.

"Oh dear, Hermia," *he fussed,* "Where have you been? I do trust that you have not failed our dear Queen. Why she has been utterly distraught ever since you flew off so recklessly without asking sensible questions like which way to go! Such manners! How could you have been so remiss …?"

But it was no good, Hermia brushed past the drone and, racing up to Queen Gertrude, spoke in such tones that the whole hive paused in its work to listen.

"Your Majesty …!"

"Yes? Why it is little Hermia!"

And, to Desmond's horror, Hermia threw her arms around the Queen and said grandly, "I believe, dear Queen Gertrude, that you asked me to bring you the pollen of the Golden Orchid?"

And Hattie could just be heard muttering, "Mark my words they'll all be doing it now!"

"Ahem," *coughed the queen.*

"Ahrmph," *muttered Desmond!* "What are you saying, Hermia, and how dare you lay hands upon Her Royal Highness in such a reckless manner? Why, the established protocol of ..."

"Oh do be quiet, Desmond!" *Gertrude said, brushing him aside.* "Let us hear what the child has to say!"

While all this was going on, all the bees had begun to notice Hermia's honey sacks and her feelers, still golden with the tell-tale grains of pollen clinging to them, and, suddenly, they all cheered. The whole hive erupted in delight. Queen Gertrude then looked down, gasped and understood. Her large face opened up in a great smile.

"Hermia, my child. What have you got there?"

"Oh, I think I forgot to tell you," *she grinned.* "I have found the pollen of the Golden Orchid."

"My dear!" *gasped Gertrude.*

"Oh, but much more," *cried Hermia.* "Much, much more!"

"Well?" *asked the queen.* "I do not imagine any work will be done today. You had better tell us."

"I am sorry. I can't stop! I must return!" *cried Hermia.* "There are some bees who need my help. They cannot possibly manage without me!"

And Hermia leapt once more into the blue, blue far yonder, to the gasps and amazement of all!

"Quick, my children, follow that bee!" *shouted Gertrude. We need some of that pollen, too.*

And a whole crowd of bees were off, over the long grasses, over bushes, past trees, and, curiously, bowling over one rather red-faced butterfly in their heady pursuit of pollen.

Finale

You may find that a frog
Will sit on a log
And just croak at the world of dreams.
He may scorn the light frond
Which grows by the pond,
So fragile and useless it seems-
It seems.
So fragile and useless it seems.

Show him the gossamer wing of a bee,
transparent, yet lifting in flight;
A shape that defies common sense, he'd see,
(If things were designed quite right-
quite right.
If things were designed quite right!)

The frog may despise
A frail butterfly's
Obsession with random delight.
He'd say – it's not snappy -
(Though, he's perfectly happy
In his improbable version of flight-
of flight.
In his improbable version of flight.)

While an ant is just smart -
Not a warm heart -
In approaching the problems of life;
It's totally efficient,
And thoroughly sufficient
And is never afraid of strife-
of strife.
It is never afraid of strife.

Yet what of a moth who's fooled by a light,
In the night,
And so senseless seems?
Who thinks it's the moon
Playing a tune
To his own private world of dreams-
of dreams.
To his own private world of dreams?

A striped fuzzing horsefly
Is really a coarse fly,
I think you will rightly agree.
He'll bother and bite,
But avoid a real fight,
For he only looks like a bee-
a bee.
He only looks like a bee.

A bright snazzy wasp
Will rarely accost
You with no provocation. You see
He's after some jam
Or pickle on ham,
And the occasional sip of tea-
                                      of tea.
The occasional sip of tea.

But a gnat, I repeat,
Is neither charming nor sweet -
As a ladybird perched on a leaf.
He'll whine and he'll hover
He'll annoy and he'll bother
You just like a small petty thief-
                                      a thief.
Just like a small petty thief.

Oh, but a bumble bee
Is both humble and free
And her visits seem gentle and kind.
You feel that her presence
Is a visit from Heaven
And that what she is seeking she'll find-
                                      she'll find.
And that what she is seeking she'll find.

The dragonfly is mysterious – why?
Ah, that would be telling, you know.
His grace and his charm
Defy any harm
Except from the 'bulgering' toad-
the toad.
Except from the 'bulgering' toad!

The snail,
Of the insect world is the whale,
So fat, so fearless and slow.
But it will nip, on the bell,
Back into its shell
At the sound of the 'peckering' crow-
the crow.
At the sound of the 'peckering' crow!

So,

From a tale such as this of wings
and things,
Some pleasant and some not so nice,
Please don't be upset
If you can't make a pet

Of a moth and a pair of woodlice-
woodlice.
Of a bee or a midge -
or a Horentious Squidge
And I certainly shan't say that twice,
not twice.
I certainly shan't say that … again!

THE END

Vocabulary

Vocabulary of special words in Quest for the Golden Orchid:

abashed	shamed
aberration	straying
adjusted	altered
aeronautics	flying skills
albeit	even though
alighted	landed upon
amiss	wrong
appalling	awful
aroma	smell
assistance	help
audience	those being entertained
availability	ease of finding
balmy	soothing
balmy	sorties uncertain attacks
battalion	large army group
bewildered	confused
blundering	clumsy
blurted out	spoke suddenly
blustered	pretended
boffins	scientists
bosun	ship's warrant officer
bulgering'	(Poetic) – bloated
	I made this one up!
bulrush	kind of reed

burly	big & sturdy
cabbage	white butterfly
capability	ability
ceremony	formal occasion
chomping	chewing
chortled	chuckled
clamouring	poetic 'shouting'
cloistered	enclosed
concealed	hidden
dank	dark & wet
debate	discussion
deliberately	on purpose
derivation	origin
deviation	not normal
disdain	scorn
dispute	argument
distraught	very upset
disuse	not in use
dithering	uncertain
divergence	separating from
dramatically	like an actor drama
droll	amusing
drone	male bee
drowsy	sleepy
dung beetle	beetle that rolls dung
emphasize	stress
erratically	uncontrolled
eventually	finally
exaggerated	magnified
files	records
flinched	twitched
flustered	panicky
follicles	cells which hold hair

fragile	delicate
functions	special work of
geometric	shape
gestures	hand signals
globule	drop of water
gossamer	thin and filmy
greengage	green plum
harvester	daddy long legs
hexagon	6-sided shape
hold court	receive admirers
honey sack	sack on bee's leg to carry pollen
host	great number (from Poem by Wordsworth)
hysterical	in panic
impaired	damaged
impetuous	rash
improbable	unlikely
in breach of	breaking (a rule)
in relation to	related to
indicating	pointing out
infer	imply
intention	purpose
marigold	yellow flower
mayfly	Long-legged insect
mission	purpose
murmured	muttered
noddle	head
obsession with random delight	self indulgent
of assistance	help
offending	displeasing
official	officer
overwhelmed	overcome
pagan	heathen

peckering'	(Poetic) – pecking
	I made this one up!
pentagon	5-sided shape
persuasively	influencing
platter	plate
pollen	yellow powder which makes honey flowers
praying mantis	insect like a big grasshopper
precariously	dangerously unbalanced
precedence	order of importance
preened	combed
profusion	great number
protocol	proper behaviour
provocation	challenging
rebuked	told off
reluctantly	unwilling
remiss	not right
resonant	vibrating
scanning	looking over
sensory	of the senses
sieved	finely separated
significance	importance
simultaneously	at the same time
staccato	short
stagnant	foul, impure
statutory	by law
strife	conflict
strumming	(Poetic) – plucking
stuttered	spoke hesitantly
surly	rude
surmise	guess
swab (the decks)	scrub nautical

swarming	bees gather in large numbers when there is a new queen
tactics	plans
time-pieces	clocks
timidly	nervously
transparent	see through
trinkets	little ornaments
unawares	not aware of
unfulfilled	not satisfied
unorthodox	unusual
vague	uncertain
veered	swerved
vile	dirty
wafting	carried on breeze
warped	bent
whimsical	fanciful

Lightning Source UK Ltd.
Milton Keynes UK
UKHW051733171019
351752UK00003B/44/P